TOMB OF TOMES

Tomb of Tomes
A Shadowbinders Story
Copyright 2026 by Andrew Watson
First Edition: January 2026
ISBN: 978-1-7393400-7-0 (Hardback)
ISBN: 978-1-7393400-8-7 (Paperback)

Cover Design by Chris Illustration
Map by Joshua Hoskins
Edited by Sarah Chorn

To Meg

For being the best writing partner anyone could ask for

Books by
Andrew Watson

The Shadowbinders Trilogy
Harbinger of Justice
The Black Mantle
Storm of Shadows

Novellas
Silence is Silver
Tomb of Tomes

TOMB OF TOMES

A Shadowbinders Story

Andrew Watson

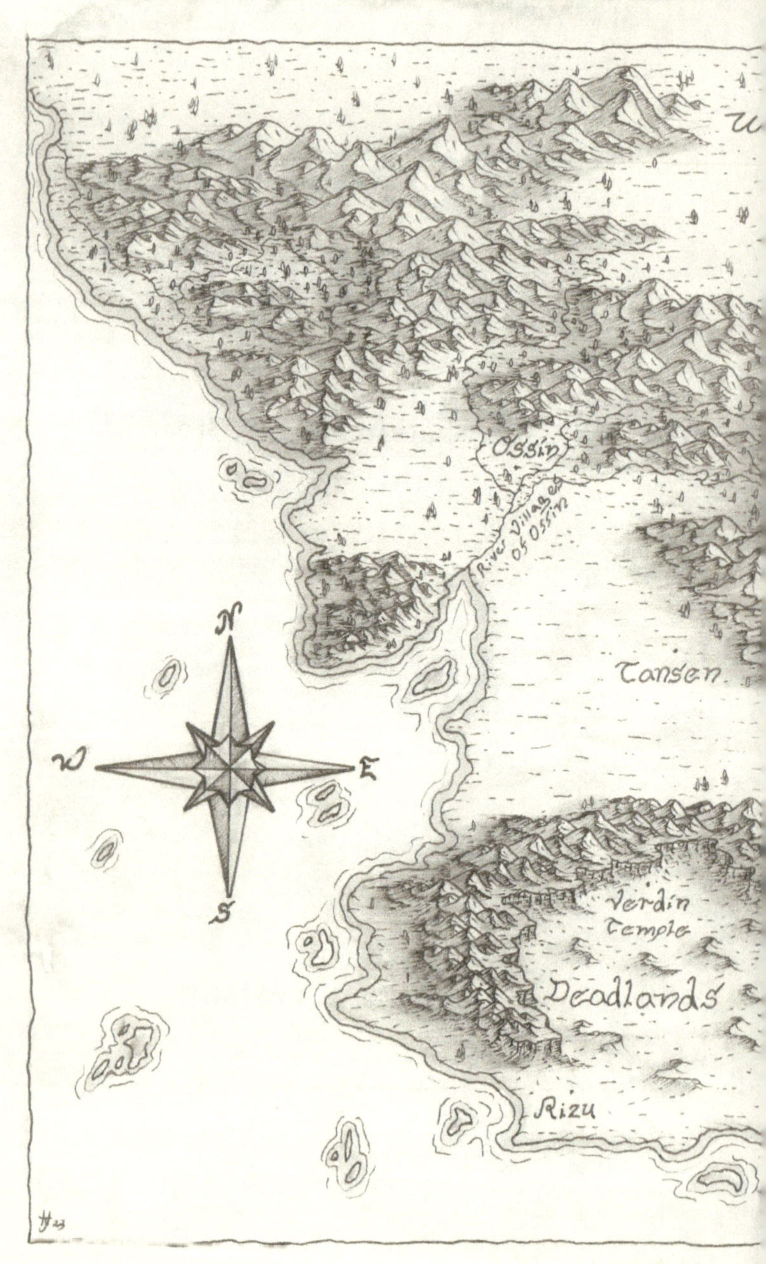

N
S
E
W
Ossin
River Village of Ossin
Tansen
Verdin Temple
Deadlands
Rizu

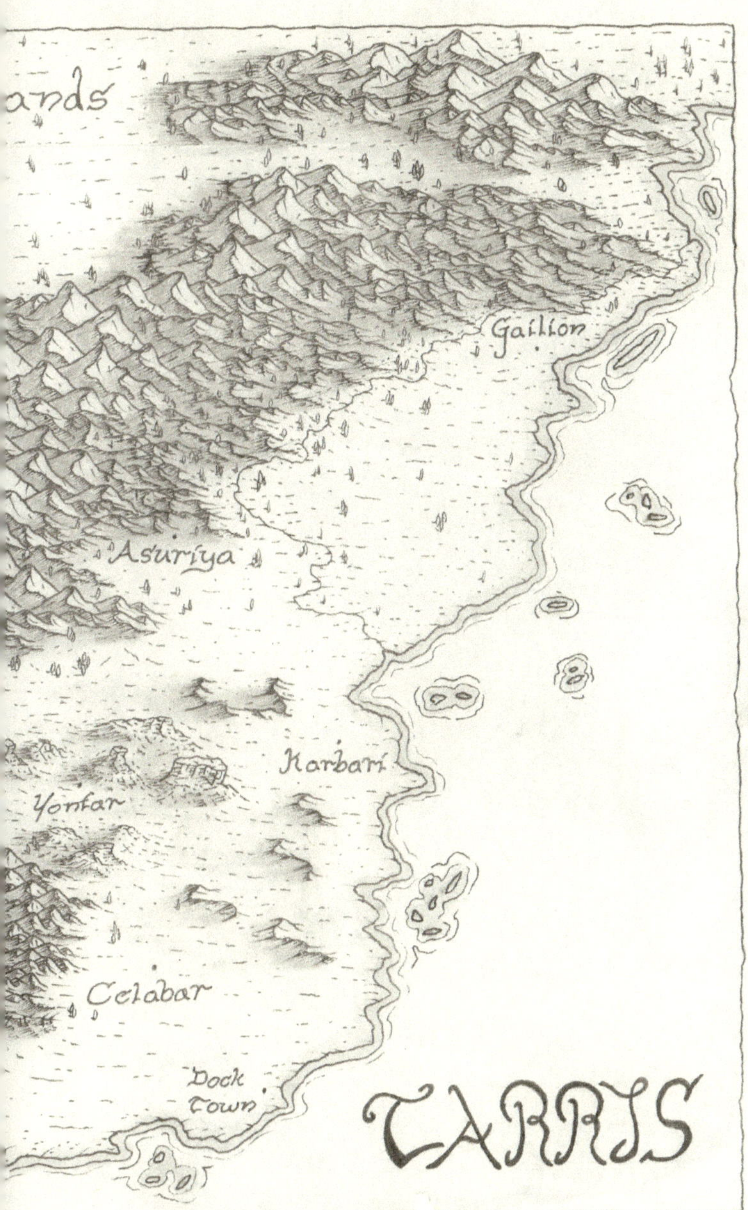

ands
Gailion
Asuriya
Karbari
Yonfar
Celabar
Dock
Town
TARRIS

1

A Site to Behold

"It is easy to disregard the many names in these ancient texts as passing mentions, forgotten a sentence later. And yet as scholars, we need to remember that these were people. They had lives, loves, desires and fears."
                                        - Yeru's Journal, page 48.

Deep within the black stone walls of the Tansen Archives, alchemical lamps shone a green pale light across the ancient shelves. The anti-burning chemical formula was the only light allowed in the Tansen Archives, painting the library in a cool emerald glow. Yeru hissed and pulled her hand back from the page edge. A drop of red dripped from her finger. She shoved her it in her mouth tasting the metallic tang of blood.

"Damn that stings," she said with her finger still in her mouth.

The small study nook in the Tansen Archives was

little more than a closet with a desk inside. But Yeru had made the most out of the space, stacking books all around her and covering the desk in scrolls. Lifting the sheet of parchment she had been writing on, Yeru held it up to the lamp and grimaced. A blotch of blood marred the corner. She couldn't very well use this now. Scholar Katri always said she used too much parchment.

She pushed it off to the side and drew a fresh sheet from the stack. With a sniff, she set about recapturing the flow of her thoughts. She had been writing about the strange markings that were found on ancient murals depicting the deity Ma-nivi. Yeru had her theories about what it meant but she needed more sources to be sure. Scholars of the past thought it was an honorific for Ma-nivi, but she wasn't so sure. The shape was curved and sharp, almost blade like, and was used when the illustration included Ma-nivi passing knowledge, not every time the deity was depicted as an honorific would dictate. So Yeru's paper hypothesized that it was a symbol for learning.

Or perhaps a way of learning, Yeru thought.

The doorway to Yeru's nook darkened.

"Shouldn't you be at Scholar Pivn's celebration?" someone asked.

Yeru glanced up and blinked. She had been staring at parchment too long and her eyes burned in the green light. Scholar Athor leant against the stone door frame, one eyebrow raised. He was one of the archive librarians that dedicated his life to the care of knowledge. He wore, what Yeru assumed was a black cloak, but she hadn't seen any librarian outside of the archive and everything within was forever tinted green in the emerald glow.

"What time is it?" Yeru asked. Her voice was hoarse after so much time unspeaking within the archive.

"The Sun Eye is soon to finish its watch," Athor said.

Was it that late already? It was so hard to track time

in the Tansen Archives as it had no windows or hints of the outside world. It was one of the reasons Yeru loved it. No distractions. Just her thoughts and the blank parchment in front of her.

If it was nearing dark hour then she would have missed the celebration meal already. Her colleagues were likely in the night theatre by now and she didn't care much for those…

"I'm in the middle of something. Maybe I'll catch up with them later," Yeru said and turned back to her work.

Scholar Athor sighed and stepped into the nook. "If I may, Yeru, you've been in here for most of the week. Can it not wait? Pivn's paper getting accepted into the archives is cause to celebrate. And a night off may help with your studies rather than hinder them."

Yeru bit her lip but didn't look up. Pivn's paper was exactly why she had to work so hard. She was happy for him but if she wanted to keep up with him, Yeru would need to publish more papers, too. Pivn and Yeru were some of the top upcoming Tansen experts on pre-cataclysm history. And she couldn't let him slip too far ahead.

"I'm not much of a night theatre person, Scholar Athor," Yeru said.

He leant across her desk, forcing Yeru to glance up.

"Nor am I but if you surround yourself in books alone, you come to realise they aren't much in the way of conversationalists."

"Maybe that's what I like about them," Yeru said.

Scholar Athor smiled. "All that wit is going to waste in here."

"Don't worry, plenty of it is being funnelled into this paper."

Another librarian appeared in the entrance and bowed to Athor. "Scholar Athor, I need you to read over these documents before they're shelved." The woman was one of the newer librarians and Yeru wasn't sure of her name.

"Drop them on my desk and I'll sort it," Athor said. The woman bowed and set off. He faced Yeru. "I should get back to work and you should be finishing up."

He closed one of the open books and Yeru yelped. "I was reading that!"

"You were, yes."

Yeru scowled at him.

"Do you want to know a secret?" Athor asked.

She stared at the closed book. Was that the tome that she was more than halfway through? Finding that exact passage again was going to be a nightmare.

"These ancient texts are magical. Truly." He lifted one of Yeru's books and inspected it in the green light. "Windows into the past and memories trapped on the page. But to know the past, you need to wander through its architecture. To know the people, you need to walk in their footsteps. You need to breathe their air."

Yeru opened her mouth.

"No," Athor said. "No quips. Save it for the party."

She closed her mouth again. Maybe he was right. She had spent most of the week in this nook, broken only by short trips back to her apartment to sleep and eat.

"Fine. But only because I want to see what the other scholars have been working on," Yeru said. She snatched the book from his hand and placed it back onto a stack.

"I'll keep the nook booked out for you," Athor said.

She nodded and stood. Yeru's knees cracked and the blood drained from her head causing the room to spin. Grabbing the desk to steady herself, she took a deep breath. Perhaps she needed to eat, too.

"Not a word," she said.

Scholar Athor lifted his hands in mock surrender.

A sharp staircase led into the *Sand's Breath* night

theatre. Yeru pulled the door open and the thick smoke of furthing leaves poured out, the alluring earthy scent pulling her into the amber-lit club. It was a smaller theatre, with the main stage in the centre of the room where acrobatic dancers rolled and swayed to the band's soft music.

"Yeru!"

Her colleagues sat around a long table on the far side of the night theatre. A cloud of furthing leaf smoke mingled with the steam of spiced teas and coffees. Yeru smiled as she approached. The girl who had called her, Isin, patted the chair beside her. She was new to the Tansen scholars and had taken a shine to Yeru. So Yeru took it upon herself to bring Isin under her wing and help her find her feet.

The others bowed as Yeru sat. She was suddenly glad Athor had persuaded her to come as the entire research team was there. They chattered and Yeru caught stray words of what they were working on currently. Each scholar had an area of expertise in Tarrisian history, occasionally collaborating with one another on a project.

"I thought you weren't going to appear!" Isin said.

Yeru smiled. "Sorry. I got caught up in the archive." Yeru leant over to Isin. "Where is Pivn?"

Isin nodded up to the coffee bar where Pivn was chatting with a woman. Yeru's rival scholar was also in his late twenties. He was the tallest amongst the scholars and was often called upon to reach the higher shelves.

Yeru squinted. Was he speaking to Overseer Sciona?

A naskh hung from Sciona's neck, the symbol of an overseer. The layered necklace was made up of many bands each representing a year that she had served in the position, and she had many. The naskh was green and gold, the green labelling her as a scholar and the gold representing the highest position an overseer could ascend to. She was the head scholar in Tansen, working directly with the empress and all the different research teams within the city.

"What is *she* doing here?" Yeru asked.

Isin drew in closer. "We're not sure. She arrived not long before you, congratulated Pivn on his paper and asked for a word. They've been at the coffee bar talking since."

The two were deep in conversation, a furrow creasing Pivn's brow. Yeru noticed others at their table stealing glances at the bar too. Pivn's paper was good. Yeru was frustrated that she hadn't made the connection between the locations of the ancient temples in cities across Tarris and how the more respected a deity was, the closer to the centre of the city their temple was built. It was a fascinating discovery pieced together from ancient journals and maps but it was hardly revolutionary. It wasn't grand enough to warrant the *head scholar* of all of Tansen to personally congratulate Pivn.

So what was this about?

"I should congratulate Pivn," Yeru said.

Isin gawked at her. "Uh, are you sure?"

"That's why we're here, right?" Yeru pushed to her feet and wandered to the bar.

As she approached, Pivn's face tightened. He clearly wasn't pleased that she was interrupting their conversation.

"Congratulations Pivn," Yeru said with a bow. "Sorry I'm late." She bowed then to the overseer. "Overseer Sciona, it's an honour to meet you."

Sciona's brown hair fell to her shoulders in even waves. She was in her early sixties with a pale complexion. And although she was shorter than Yeru, Sciona had an air of confidence that made Yeru uneasy.

Pivn rubbed his temple. "Thank you, Yeru."

"Scholar Yeru, we were just talking about you," Sciona said.

"Talking about me?" A flush burned Yeru's cheeks and her voice came out higher than she meant it to.

Her discomfort seemed to amuse Sciona and a smile curled the edges of her mouth. "Yes. Scholar Katri assures me that you two are the finest young scholars in pre-cataclysm history." Sciona cleared her throat and lowered her voice. "And well, I have been looking for some such as yourselves. There has been two new sites recently discovered that may need your expertise."

"New discoveries?" Yeru asked, too loudly.

Sciona glared at her. "This is secret. I don't want a word of this conversation breathed to anyone."

"Yes, Overseer." Yeru bowed, her face reddening further.

"I said I can handle them, Overseer Sciona," Pivn said.

Sciona crossed her arms. "And how do you plan to be at two sites at once?"

"I'll visit one then the other," Pivn said. "Yeru has no site experience. Send me. You'd rather stay here anyway, right Yeru?"

They both stared at her. Yeru sucked in a breath. It was true. She hadn't been on any sites that weren't pre-established and well researched. New sites posed risks and she was a scholar, not an adventurer.

"I…"

"Before you say a word, I want to make this very clear. I can't discuss the sites here." Sciona waved to the night theatre around her. "But if the messenger's claims turn out to be true, this will change everything we know about pre-cataclysm history. These *are* potentially dangerous sites, and not just from the sites themselves. So I need two young up and comers to be the first on the scene."

Change everything?

Yeru's mind was a whirl. What could they have found?

"What do you mean not just the sites themselves?" Pivn whispered.

Sciona cleared her throat. "Between us, a discovery

like this will be huge. And word will no doubt have already reached the other cities."

The overseer didn't need to finish the thought. If this was as big as she was claiming, there would be interest from every scholar in Tarris, all wanting to slap their name on the discovery for the sake of their city and careers.

Yeru nodded in understanding. "Where are the sites?"

"North of Yontar. One a couple days ride into the desert and the other is on the outskirts of Asuriya," Sciona said.

So far, Yeru thought. She had read every piece of literature on Asuriya, the lost capital of Tarris that she could find. It was the reason she focused her research on pre-cataclysm history. She wanted to know what caused the event in their history that turned their ancient capital city into a sandstone skeleton and infected the creatures and landscape around it with the blight.

It was well known that wildlife around the city had changed and become blight-touched. Travellers avoided getting too close to Asuriya as the creatures were dangerous and unpredictable. Sciona couldn't expect them to go to the outskirts, surely.

"Asuriya is one of the most treacherous places in Tarris," Pivn said.

"I wouldn't send you alone," Sciona said. "A company of guards and a personal assistant each."

An entire company of guards? What threats was the head scholar expecting them to come across? Yeru hadn't even been on a new site, much less one with this level of potential danger. "I... I don't know if I can do this, Overseer," Yeru said.

Sciona offered Yeru a disappointed look and then nodded. "The decision is yours, Scholar Yeru. I will give you until tomorrow evening to decide. If not, Pivn, you can travel between the sites."

Tomorrow evening? This was all so fast.

"Thank you, Overseer," Pivn said. He bowed. "When do I leave?"

"Come to me tomorrow and I will tell you more about the site and what is expected of you. Then you will leave come dark hour."

Pivn choked on his drink. "So soon?"

"Time is of the essence. And you will speak to no one of this." She pointedly looked between the two of them until they both nodded. "Good. Congratulations again on your paper, Scholar Pivn."

Pivn stammered out a thank you as the overseer pushed past them and left the night theatre. For a moment, they both just stared at the door before turning to one another.

"This is big," Pivn said and then took a swig of his tea.

"What do you think they've found?" Yeru asked.

"I don't know. A temple perhaps? The site on the outskirts of Asuriya has to be something important," Pivn muttered more to himself than Yeru. "I'll go there first."

He pat Yeru on the back. "Thank you for coming and don't worry about the sites. There's no shame in remaining here and continuing your studies. Perhaps I'll be back in time to celebrate one of your papers getting into the archives."

With that, he stalked back to their table, receiving a cheer as he sat. Yeru bit the inside of her lip.

The rest of the night was an incoherent whirl. She couldn't focus on the conversation. All she could think about was these new sites and the secrets they could hold.

2

True Stories

"I try to see through the eyes of the dead, hear through their ears."

- Yeru's Journal, page 151.

"That's amazing, Yeru!" her mother, Teth, said. Yeru should have known visiting her mother was going to end with a meal. She never could escape the place without being fed. Her traitorous stomach growled as she watched Teth fill a bowl with steaming soup.

Yeru's parents lived in a small home on the eastern side of Tansen. It was close to the merchant district at the gate to the city, which had been helpful for her father when he returned from his travels with goods to sell.

Teth placed the bowl down in front of Yeru and sat beside her. "It is good news, isn't it?" She looked at Yeru with her all-knowing eyes.

"It is," Yeru said not meeting her gaze.

"Then why do you look so forlorn?"

"I don't look *forlorn*, Mother," Yeru said. "I just…
I don't know if it's a good idea. It's dangerous and I
won't be able to swing by and see you and… and my
papers. I can't very well continue my studies if this site
is taking up all my time."

Teth raised a questioning eyebrow. "Your papers?"

It sounded silly when she said it like that. Yeru stammered out some noises as she tried to find the words to
explain it.

"Is this about your father?" Teth asked.

"What? No! I mean, kind of. He isn't here and if I'm
not either, then…" Yeru trailed off. A hand clasped
Yeru's shoulder and squeezed lightly.

"He'll be back, Yeru, and I'm fine."

"I know. I just… I don't want to disappear and leave
you too," Yeru said.

Her father was a merchant and he travelled across
the seas to places Yeru could only dream of. Lands like
the Trosan Empire in the frozen north, like the Ekrine
Forest with the ever-growing tree. But he always came
home when he said he would.

Except this time.

What was supposed to be a short trip lasting a
month, had now been close to a year. And they had no
word from him. Before Yeru had moved out, she had
checked with the wall guard every day. But there had
been no sightings and no word from him.

"Your father is more than a travelling merchant, you
know this." She smiled at Yeru. "He's an adventurer.
He'll be caught up in some mess that only he can solve.
But he'll be back. He always comes back."

"I know… I—" Yeru took a breath.

"Please Yeru don't stay for me. If this is what you
want then you need to chase it," Teth said.

"I don't know if I can be like him. I love hearing
about his stories but from *here*. From the safety of

our home." Yeru swirled her spoon through her soup watching the reddish-brown liquid ripple out to the edge of the bowl.

Teth laughed. "You don't think you can be like him?" Teth lifted Yeru's head up and grabbed her cheek. "You're his spitting image, Yeru. Minus the stubble that he's too lazy to shave."

A smile bled onto Yeru's face and then Teth's expression grew serious.

"That passion in your heart and that fire in your eyes. That's his. I can see it burning away in there. That. That is what your father is like, and that is what you're like. The daughter of a bookkeeper and a travelling merchant, you are the best of us both and so much more," Teth said.

Yeru smiled and said, "Maybe you should write my papers."

"If it was numbers and statistics sure. But those stories and the past you dredge up, that's all you and your father," Teth said. "Now, eat your soup."

Her father's study was a clutter of book stacks and trinkets. Treasures, as he called them. The small window was half covered in parchment of pinned up notes letting in a diffused warm light painting strips across the map on the wall.

Yeru ran a finger over the shelves. She carefully stepped past the too-high stacks of books to his desk that was a mess of more notes. She held her breath, easing between the wall and the desk and then dropped into his chair. The cushion puffed out a cloud of dust.

The last note on his desk was a hurried scribble. Yeru could barely read his handwriting but it was a list of items he had yet to pack for his trip. She picked up the rough parchment. He had been in such a hurry to leave.

"Where are you?" she whispered.

They had sat right here when Yeru realised that she

wanted to become a historian. She had been on his lap while he read her a story.

"Do you see this?" her father had asked. A book was laid out in front of them depicting a thunder cloud with a dark shape within. Yeru nodded.

"What do you think it is?" her father asked.

"A monster?" a six-year-old Yeru asked.

Her father laughed, it was a bright sound that filled the room. "I suppose it is. And this?" He turned the page to another illustration, this time of a huge bird flying across a battlefield.

"Nightraven!" Yeru said.

"That's right!" Her father rustled her hair. "I've told you stories about them before, haven't I? But do you know what's special about these stories? These books in here?" He gestured to the study around them.

Yeru shook her head.

"Well, these are more than stories. They aren't like the stories you hear from the other children," he said.

"Why?"

"Well because these" —he patted on the book—"stories are true. Nightravens once flew through the skies. The monsters once roamed the desert sand." He clasped his arms around Yeru's shoulder and tapped his fingers like a monster coming to get her. Yeru laughed and pushed him off.

"But that also means the heroes are true, too. They were there." He grew solemn as he flicked through the pages of the book. "It means the magic was there. *Is* here in Tarris. These stories are special, Yeru, because they are filled with magic that we can still find if we look hard enough."

Yeru wasn't sure when the tears had started but she wiped them away as the memory faded.

Resolve hardened like the black sands of night. She could do this. It was what she wanted to do.

Pushing the chair back, Yeru reached under the desk and slid out a drawer. She pressed her fingers down the side of the stacks of parchment to its base and felt for the familiar notch. She yanked it up and the false base lifted to reveal a dagger. The blade itself was black with a silver pommel inlaid with black trim. Yeru lifted it and slid it into her belt.

It was time to dig up those tales.

Upon arriving at the Tansen Palace gates, Yeru was admitted quickly, the guards saying that they had been expecting her. A guide led her through the palace to the scholars' wing.

Yeru stepped into the grandest study she had ever seen. The far wall was more glass than stone. A curved wooden desk lay bare at its feet and Scholar Sciona was walking among the many shelves that stretched into the left side of the room. *It's like a personal library*, Yeru thought.

The head scholar glanced up as Yeru entered and smiled. "I was wondering when I'd see you."

Yeru bowed. "I'd like to take you up on your offer of establishing one of the sites, Scholar Sciona."

With a thwack, Sciona slammed shut the book she had been reading and slid it back onto the shelf. "I knew you would. Come, sit."

She gestured to the plush cushioned chairs around a circular table off to one side, rather than her desk. So Yeru wandered over and sat.

"Tea?" Sciona asked as she eased into the chair across from Yeru.

"No, thank you," Yeru said.

Sciona nodded and turned to the servant at the door. "Just one, Vint." And the man sped off out of the study.

"So you've changed your mind." Sciona clasped her fingers over her lap.

"Yes, head scholar. I have been thinking and I don't want fear to dictate my choices."

"Wise words. Wiser still to see that it was fear creeping into your thoughts. Few are able to make that distinction."

The servant returned and placed a steaming mug in front of Sciona before bowing and stepping back outside of the room.

"Now," Sciona said as she lifted her cup and sipped. "I've already assigned Pivn to Ma-atan's temple."

"Ma-atan's temple?" Yeru's eyes went wide. There were plenty of temples dedicated to the deity of justice throughout Tarris but a simple place of worship wouldn't call for the secrecy and head scholar's involvement. "So that must mean…" Yeru started.

"Yes. We believe the Scale Council Chamber has been found, where the Judgings took place. And perhaps the very resting place of the deity."

That was impossible. Ma-atan was said to be there when one died, to Judge their lives. There were those that believed the deity was once in the land of the living, as there were ancient scripts that could be interpreted that way. Yeru remembered reading a paper years ago from a low-ranking scholar called Kyan about how mythology could have formed over thousands of years, and that deities might once have been creatures with incredible power, not gods at all. It had been a fascinating read but little evidence was there to back up the theories.

This discovery would revolutionize how they thought of deities. Most modern day Tarrisians believed them to be nothing more than symbols.

"With Pivn's recent research and focus on deities and temples, I thought he would be best suited to the site," Sciona said. She leant over the table then. "But Scholar Katri spoke of your impressively broad knowledge of pre-cataclysm history. And how you seem to have read books and scrolls on all kinds of topics."

"I do read widely," Yeru said. And it was true. To get a better picture of how Tarris had been, she had to be all-encompassing and read anything she could get her hands on.

A grin spread across Sciona's face. "Then the second site is perfect for you. If the early reports are to be believed, we may have found the lost library of Nenelan."

Everything stilled. The very dust motes seemed to freeze.

The lost library of Nenelan was thought to be a myth. A grand library that contained knowledge from before the cataclysm that destroyed their old capital was too good to be true. And the few times it was mentioned within ancient texts, the library was different. It was a refuge of knowledge in some, where truth flourished away from the prying eyes of evil. In others it was the epicentre of Tarrisian culture, where anyone could come and go. Not to mention the contradicting locations of where the library had been.

Because of this dispute, few scholars believed the library had ever existed. Expeditions had taken place and Yeru had read the reports but none had turned up anything. She thought it fanciful to have this wealth of untouched knowledge of pre-cataclysm Tarris.

But if it were real they could finally find out the truth of what Tarris was like back then and perhaps even what caused the fall of Asuriya and splintering of their country all those thousands, if not tens of thousands, of years ago.

Yeru realised she had been staring blankly at the scholar for some time.

"I thought that might pique your interest," Sciona said.

"Is it true?"

Sciona shrugged. "That's what you're tasked with finding out. I don't think I need to tell you the importance of a discovery like this. We do not know what the library could hold, both in the way of traps and creatures but also the knowledge itself.

"A wise friend of mine, Overseer Lieten once said, *a sword can kill a man but parchment can raze empires.*" Sciona let that settle in.

"And there is something else," Sciona said.

"The greatest font of knowledge has possibly been discovered and you're telling me there is more?" Yeru clasped a hand over her mouth. Had she really spoken to the head scholar like that?

Sciona tapped her fingers on the table seeming not to notice Yeru's flippant tone. "What I told you at the night theatre is true, there are other parties at play here in Tarris. Of course there are the competitive scholars that want to claim the discovery as their own. But there are also some that want to control the narrative. They want to carefully choose what is known and what should remain buried."

The room tipped off its axis as a flush rose from Yeru's gut in a sickly wave. She knew of the scholars that cared only about their careers but to hear that there were some who wanted to hide the truth, wasn't something she had considered.

"Who would want to hide the past? The other monarchs?" Yeru asked.

Sciona waved a hand. "No, no, no. Nothing so blatant. There is a group that we've run into before at ancient sites. They have strange and passionate beliefs about some less favourable deities."

When it was clear that Yeru wasn't satisfied with that answer, Sciona cleared her throat and continued. "They think that the cataclysm could have been used to bury secrets. Things we should not know. And so, they have tried to stop us from uncovering more about the past. They will likely be at the site with you, hidden with the rest of the scholars, guards, and personal assistants. But fear not. They are rarely violent and the guards I will send with you are most definitely not part of their... cult."

If the head scholar meant that to be reassuring, it wasn't working. Panic seeped into Yeru and she felt the urge to look around, as if this cult might be hiding among the shelves in Sciona's study.

"You will be perfectly safe. But I want you to know the situation before agreeing and setting off. I need someone like you there, Yeru. Someone passionate about the truth. Someone I can trust is there for the right reasons."

Yeru was honoured by the head scholar's words but this was a heavier task than she could have ever anticipated.

"And you want… me to do this?" Yeru asked.

Sciona leant over the table and clasped Yeru's hand. "I have been following you closely. I can see the passion and cleverness in your work. I know I'm asking a lot. I would go myself if I could but I need someone smarter and younger."

"This is a lot," Yeru said.

"It is. But time is of the essence. I need you to decide now. Others will already be travelling to the site as we speak."

The daughter of a bookseller and an adventurer. Yeru had always felt that she had more of her mother in her. And yet the sense of possibilities prickled the hairs on her arm.

"I'll do it."

3

Sand and Scrolls

"As I work through memoirs and journals I'm reminded of how different, not only how the world was, but how differently they saw it."

\- Yeru's Journal, page 62.

Sitting under a tarp aback an aya in the scorching desert, Yeru missed her reading nook. Sweat beaded on her brow as she squinted at her notes. It dripped down her face and splashed against the parchment. Yeru bit her lip thinking of the cool of the Tansen Archive. And as she made note of a reference that she wanted to look up later, Yeru missed having Tarris' historical records at her fingertips.

Isin stretched, the top half of her body poking out into the Sun Eye's gaze. Her eyes were closed, light brown hair a cushion beneath her head as she basked in the glow. Scholar Sciona had let Yeru bring along one assistant as well as her company of guards. While

Isin was new and perhaps not the best pick for a trip as important as this, with less experience than most of her colleagues, Yeru needed the familiarity. She needed someone she knew at her side and Isin was the closest she had to a friend amongst the scholars.

Some sixth sense made Isin open her eyes and she smiled at Yeru. "It's nice being out of the city, isn't it?" she asked.

"It's a little hot," Yeru said running a hand over her forehead to catch the sweat. "Not the best conditions for research."

"We will be studying in the library for months. Why don't you come relax with me for a bit? Make the most of the fresh air." Isin patted the spot beside her.

Yeru blew out a breath. "I need to work through these notes about the library. I want to go in as prepared as I can be. There's so much to read and none of it connects with the rest," Yeru said flicking through her notes.

Isin crawled over and dropped down beside Yeru, looking over her shoulder at the notebook.

"See here." Yeru pointed to a passage.

"The library of Nenelan was well frequented by all. It was more than a place of knowledge but the heart of Tarris. Librarians were not only scholars but guides. They sat with the people and spoke with them about life and ones place in it," Yeru read.

"However, if we look at this account," Yeru said picking up a leather tome. The binding had been restored within the archives but Yeru still took care to peel back the pages.

"The library of Nenelan is our last bastion of hope. It sits beneath the world as a place free of darkness. It is our last light and our safe haven," Yeru read.

Isin bit her lip. "When are these from?"

"From the best we can tell, they're both from before the cataclysm. The first account is slightly older but by how much, we can't tell," Yeru said.

"Could they both be true?" Isin asked.

"I suppose. You think it was a centre of Tarris and then something happened forcing it to become this *'bastion of hope'*?" Yeru asked.

Isin shrugged. "Maybe." She stretched back out into the sunlight. "If this site really is the library, we might get answers soon enough."

Sand and time trickled by, and Yeru grew to enjoy the travel. Golden sand replaced the dark walls of the Tansen Archive. The emerald glow of the alchemical lamps were traded for pale light of the Sun Eye. But there were few distractions and Yeru found that she could sink into her studies. Drawn through the portal of parchment, Yeru fell through a fragmented ancient Tarris. There she filled in gaps like an artist adding to a mural, piecing together what little they knew of those times.

The days passed in a flurry of gold and soon they had arrived at Yontar, the last stop before heading north to the research site and possibly a place thought to be nothing more than myth.

They passed through the gates of Yontar. Yeru and Isin atop the aya and six guards surrounding them on hyianback. The morning markets lined the streets with garish tarps pulled over the many stalls. Merchants bartered with customers waving their hands around theatrically. Yeru twitched her nose against the pungent mix of spices.

Ahead, the Thousand Floor Palace stood above it all. A layered tower that rose high into the sky. Yeru could make out movement on some of the lower-level balconies, like ants scuttling through an ant hill.

Isin peered over the edge of their platform, eyes wide.

"Is this your first time in Yontar?" Yeru asked.

Isin nodded without turning. "The palace is so… large." She faced Yeru and her face flushed. "That was a stupid thing to say. I'm sorry. Of course it's big. I just didn't think it would be *that* big."

Yeru laughed. "It is quite a sight. My father took me here as a child and I thought much the same."

Isin settled beside Yeru as the aya tromped on through the city streets, guided by the guards around them.

"I thought it might look less colossal now as an adult but I was wrong," Yeru said.

The aya was led into the courtyard of the Cartographer's inn. The guards talked with the stable hands as Yeru and Isin passed inside to get out of the heat and purchase their rooms.

The scent of mildew wafted out of the door as they entered. High backed chairs were laid around tables and freestanding bookshelves broke the common room up into segments. A huge map of the world covered the far wall. Yeru stepped up to it mouth agape. It was so detailed that she could make out individual peaks in the Bandor Mountain range. The common room closer resembled a study than an inn.

The innkeeper nodded as Yeru approached the bar. He was an older gentleman with short grey hair that blended into the stubble on his chin.

"Can we have a room for two, please?" Yeru asked.

"Sure thing." The innkeeper retrieved a key from beneath the countertop and handed it over. "Is there some meeting on I should know about?" he asked.

Yeru raised an eyebrow.

The man shrugged. "You're the second lot of scholars staying here, is all."

Yeru's lips drew into a line. They were likely other scholars heading to the same site. "What did they look like?" Yeru asked.

The innkeeper gestured to the far side of the common room. Yeru's stomach dropped as she saw the party sitting in a booth in the corner. Scholars from Rizu. Yeru recognised several of them from gatherings in Tansen. And among those faces, Yeru met eyes with Etan. A grin sprouted on the man's face.

Yeru turned towards the staircase, leading Isin with a hand on her back when Etan called, "Yeru?"

She closed her eyes and took a deep breath before mustering up a fake smile and making her way over to the table. Isin watched her with concern but didn't say a word.

"Yeru, that is you!" Etan said. The Rizu scholar sat with two of his colleagues, each with their own assistants. The low light of the lamps warmed his brushed back black hair.

"Etan, nice to see you again," Yeru said.

"And you. So far away from home, too." Etan gave her a knowing smile. "You know my friends here, Diven and Erid." They each nodded. Yeru noted that he didn't introduce the three assistants. He had always been an arrogant man.

"And who is this?" Etan asked looking at Isin.

Yeru stepped to the side. "This is my friend, Isin."

"Nice to meet you," Isin said in a quiet voice.

"And you," Etan said.

"Now, we really must get settled in. We have been travelling for weeks," Yeru said as she bowed.

"Of course, of course. We will no doubt be seeing more of one another in the coming weeks anyway," Etan said.

Yeru forced a smile and led Isin away from their table. They made their way up the narrow staircase and into a long corridor.

"Of course Etan is here," Yeru muttered as she fumbled for the key.

"Who are they?" Isin asked.

"Rizu scholars. And some of the most arrogant people you will ever meet." The lock clicked and the door swung open.

The room was austere with a bed on either side of the room and a chest at the foot of each. The shuttered window was closed, keeping the room cool from the burning gaze of the Sun Eye. Still, that fiery warmth outlined the edges of the frame in white hot lines.

Yeru rubbed at her face as she dropped her bag beside the chest.

"They must be headed to the site too," Isin said.

That was likely. And if the scholars from Rizu had made it all the way to Yontar, then those from Ossin and Yontar may have already arrived at the library. Scholar Sciona had hoped that they could avoid any leaks until Yeru and Pivn arrived at the sites but that clearly hadn't worked.

"Get some sleep. We need to leave at dark hour," Yeru said.

Yeru didn't know what to expect but a simple cave entrance was not high on her list of probabilities. She had seen a thousand other caves like it. Inside the cavern's entrance was the remnants of a camp with blackened stone where fits pits were once lit. Refuse and discarded belongings lay tucked around the edges of the cave.

Yeru leant down and rubbed ash between her fingers. "This must be from those who found the site."

They had been told that a party had settled in the cavern to avoid a sandstorm. For unknown reasons, part of the group delved deeper into the cave and found what they believed to be the library. *What a fortunate turn of events*, Yeru thought as the cave was north of Yontar in a stretch of desert that so few travelled.

Guards surrounded Yeru and Isin as they pushed further into the dark. They held aloft torches pushing back the murk of unknown and painting the passage around them with a warm glow.

"Of all the places to find the lost library of Nenelan this seems… strange," Isin said. Her voice bounced around the stalactites above.

Yeru was thinking the same thing. A cave in the

middle of the desert? Why would the library have been here? They were on the outskirts of Asuriya, so perhaps a village had once been here? But that didn't explain the simple cave entrance. She would have thought they would find statues and some hint of human touch.

"We should have an excavation team go over the land around the cave entrance," Yeru said.

Isin nodded.

It wasn't long before they came across the sandfall. It wasn't a surprise as it had been in the report Scholar Sciona gave them. The hiss of the ever-flowing sand filled the quiet. Raised torches revealed the constant flow of sand covering the back wall of the cave. It was common in ancient times to have a way of weakening those entering places of importance. Often it was sharp stones to prick ones finger with. Yeru hadn't read of a sandfall being used before in the practice but it worked in the same way. Scholars theorised that thousands of years ago they had more extreme measures to ensure places like the library of Nenelan remained a violence free zone but over time these practices softened to the point that they became more symbolic, rather than incapacitating.

One of the guards pushed through first. He grunted as he passed through the sandfall. Yeru reached out and the cutting sand bit into her fingertips. She yelped, pulling back.

"Is there any way to stop the sandfall?" Isin asked.

"Unlikely," Yeru said. "These doorways were built so that they were unavoidable."

Isin screwed her face up. "We can manage a few cuts," Yeru said and patted Isin's shoulder.

Putting on a brave face, Yeru leapt through the sand. Cuts and scrapes flared across her body as she burst out the other side. Pain blossomed like a swarm of insects had stung her. She hissed and dabbed her wounds as Isin and the other guards passed through.

She had been so caught up with the stinging that it took her a second to realise the change in lighting. The chamber around them was lit in a pale light. Not the dancing flames or the green hue of the alchemical lamps back in the Tansen Archive but the neutral light of day.

White glowing orbs were mounted onto the walls of a grand cavern and ornate patterns decorated the tiles. Rows of benches were cut out of the stone and faced a grand mural centred with a huge open door. Other scholars and guards milled around the space, inspecting the room with notebooks and handheld brushes used to wipe off dust.

Yeru couldn't believe her eyes. It was all so well preserved. She stepped up to the wall and ran a finger over the red tile. "Even the colours are still vivid."

"Yeru," Isin said pointing towards the mural. Among the different panels of illustrations was Ma-nivi, deity of knowledge. The owl-like being had large eyes and wings that it wrapped around itself. It was often found at places of learning. Only then did Yeru realise she hadn't truly believed that the site was the lost library of Nenelan until now. But this was unlike anything she had ever seen. Awe warmed her with a flush of anticipation and she grabbed one of the benches to steady herself.

"Quite something, isn't it?" A woman stood at Yeru's side smiling at the mural. "Wait until you get a closer look. The detail is unfathomable."

The woman had white hair that was pulled back into a ponytail and she wore light and airy trousers, contrasting the tight long-sleeved top.

Yeru was about to bow but then saw the notebook under her arm. *A scholar with such rich fabrics?* Yeru wondered.

"Scholar Whute from Rizu." She tipped her head.

"Scholar Yeru. Tansen," Yeru said matching the gesture. So her hunch was right and the other scholars were already here. She needed to find Isin and do a quick canvas of the area to note all the different schol- ar groups that had beaten them to the site. Yeru spun around to see Isin standing at one of the white orbs chatting away with another scholar. That was good. Isin had an easy going charm to her that made others open up. She would find answers of who all was here soon enough.

"We have set up a camp inside," Whute said.

Yeru raised an eyebrow. "Inside?"

A devilish grin spread across Whute's face. "Follow me."

She led Yeru through the chamber to the grand door at the back of the cavern. A golden root design covered the door and handles. Yeru stopped and felt the pro- truding design work. It was metal.

"We think they smelted the metal down. But how they got the final product so precise, we aren't sure," Whute said standing in the door frame.

Yeru nodded. "Roots to indicate the foundation of society and the sharing of knowledge as the roots spread outward."

"I hadn't thought of that," Whute said. There was surprise in her tone. "You have a keen eye, Scholar Yeru."

A sweet earthy scent wafted through the short corri- dor past the door. The musty smell of books eroding. The smell of knowledge decaying. Yeru knew she should abhor the scent of most ancient places. It was the death of what she searched for and yet she could never hate the almost vanilla-like aroma. It was famil- iar and comforting.

They stepped out into an open area, where tents had been erected. No campfires, Yeru noted gratefully. They would need to cook far from here to preserve the area.

Past the camp was a wonder that belonged in myth. Bookshelves rose high above them, filled with ancient tomes. Yeru pushed through the camp, ignoring the stares from the other scholars and guards and stepped up to the balustrade. She peered down an endless void. There had to be hundreds of floors leading to an unseen bottom. Above her, a giant white orb was surrounded in spinning metal bars. It was much like those smaller orbs in the chamber outside but this one was at least a storey tall and hovering above the drop. Yeru squinted to try and spot cables but saw nothing. It was just *floating* there.

Despite the activity behind her, Yeru heard the faint hum come from that orb. How was it floating and what was creating that light? To still be lit after thousands of years was incomprehensible. There was no alchemical mix or fuel that was known that could create such a bright and long lasting illumination.

Yeru's hands tightened around the stone railing. If there had been any doubt of this being the lost library of Nenelan, it eroded then. Washed away in the awe of the place. It was grander than she could have ever imagined. Of course, the myths spoke of its incredible size. But they were just that, myths. This place couldn't exist.

And yet, it did.

Mind a whirl of thought, Yeru slid her parchment out of her belt and began to write.

4

The Scholarly Pursuit

"You see in all times across history that most war and death can be traced back to a quiet room, where safe and comfortable nobles sip on tea and decide the fate of millions."
\- Yeru's Journal, page 34.

The map of Tarris was carved into the stone wall of the library. Mountains were cut into the rock and cities and towns, many lost to the ages, were labelled in the old tongue. There was Lophut, a city that stood tens of thousands of years ago known for its towers of silver and gold before being razed to rubble by war. And across the middle of the map was a route. A path that cut through Tarris in a large circle, passing all the major cities.

The library of Nenelan moved.

This was why there were so many discrepancies with the location in historical records. They weren't mistakes or mistranslations, they were all right. How ancient Tarrisians were able to move such a massive structure, Yeru had no idea. And none of the other scholars had theories on the feat either.

She had spoken little to the others in the hours she had roamed the entryway to the library. The scholars were polite and forthcoming while still reserved. That was fine with Yeru.

Following up on the anonymous tip, the first scholars that had arrived at the library were juniors from Yontar. Messages from weary travellers about incredible findings were common and often nothing more than strange rock formations. So few took the tip seriously. This was until the scholars reached the site and sent word that it was true. Then the others flocked like vultures to a kiren's carcass.

Few had delved deeper into the library, for many reasons. The first being that there was so much to see in the entryway. One could spend weeks studying the details in the chamber outside alone. Another was that creatures had been spotted among the stacks of books and there was a consensus that there could be dangerous animals within the library. Biologists noted the effects of closed ecosystems and that they were to tread lightly. Unknown plant life had been found growing from the bookshelves by the entrance, so what they would find floors down was a mystery.

An Ossin scholar ignored the warnings and his party had travelled down to the lower floors several days before Yeru's arrival but they had yet to reappear, further discouraging the others from exploring deeper into the lost library.

Yeru sketched the map on the wall, noting all the major settlements and places where the library stopped. She would need to send word to Sciona to send parties to investigate each site. Yeru knew she was playing catch up with some of the other scholars and they likely had teams searching for the other stops already.

"Hey, I've sent up the tent. You should come and eat

something."

Yeru turned too quickly and the room fell off its axis. She wavered before Isin caught her.

"Wow, careful," Isin said. She eased her down to the ground and handed her a waterskin. "You can't forget to care for yourself."

Sipping at the waterskin, the room settled around Yeru. She supposed she had been forgetting to drink and eat. And rest.

Isin searched the corner of her eyes before drawing closer. "I've found out as much as I can. I'll tell you over food."

Yeru kept her intrigue from lighting up her face. She knew she could trust Isin to learn more from the other scholars. She had always been better with people than Yeru.

Isin pulled Yeru to her feet. It was only now, with the mention of food that her stomach growled. "Let's go eat, then."

Tucked into the second row of bookshelves, the guards and Isin had set up their tents on the outskirts of the scholars' camps. Any food was to be cooked outside by the rows of benches to avoid any flames or smoke in the library. But most scholars set up their tents and base of operations inside the entrance.

Yeru dropped onto a cushion across from Isin who fished out some dried meats and breads. As she laid them out on the low table, Yeru asked, "So what did you find out?"

"Well," Isin dragged the word out, "The scholars from Ossin seem to stick their tongues out when concentrating."

Yeru raised an eyebrow and Isin grinned.

"I'm kidding. Well, I'm not. They do. But I learnt more than that." She shuffled forward and lowered her voice. "All of the major research groups are here; Ossin, Rizu, Yontar, and of course us. But there are smaller scholar groups here too. Three by my count."

As well as most major cities having teams of scholars that were sent out to sites, there were a few well-funded research groups in outer cities or even in the major cities but acting as separate entities from the city's own that had formed over the years.

"And how is the dynamic?" Yeru asked.

Isin swallowed a piece of bread and shrugged. "Depends on who you ask. They're not stabbing each other in their sleep, if that's what you're asking."

Yeru had told Isin of Sciona's warning about this cult and their threats. Normally with big discoveries like this, the one who found it took the credit. However, in strange cases where someone stumbled across it and sent word to the scholars, the acclaim of finding it is thrown to the wind and so scholars clamoured for the first big discovery at the site to become the individual who is written about in the histories. Which meant new sites could become hostile places. It had been over one hundred years since a scholar had killed another scholar over a discovery. However, tampering with others' research, hiding discoveries and outright lying about theories to send others down the wrong path was common in these situations.

"Well I suppose that's a start," Yeru said.

Isin shuffled closer. "Are you going to tell me more about Etan now?" She had continued to pester Yeru about the other scholar since they had met in Yontar. Isin assumed there was some history there.

"There's nothing to tell. We met at a gathering in Tansen and found out that we were both writing a paper on pre-cataclysm worship and sacrificial rituals. Needless to say, neither of us were pleased that the other was working on the paper so it created somewhat of a rivalry."

"And who won? Who got their paper out first?"

Yeru smiled. "Who do you think?"

Isin grinned back.

"However, that will only push him harder to find something notable here," Yeru said. "Have you heard any whispers about discoveries?"

"Small things. Nothing big yet. Some say they are close to a breakthrough but it's hard to tell if they're saying that just to slow and redirect other scholars." Isin rolled her eyes. "It reminds me of my school days. Who would have thought there would be more drama amongst the most well-read people in all of Tarris than in a school."

Yeru scoffed. She was right. What Yeru found was that a lot of traits in children were in some adults too, they were just more complex and better hidden.

They sat in silence eating for a while. The furious scratch of quills and hushed conversations echoed around the high ceiling. Yeru still couldn't believe she was in the lost library of Nenelan. *The secrets it must hold,* she mused. And yet she saw how deep the floors went. A lot of the literature around this entrance were directories to find certain wings of the library on specific topics. And if they were anything to go by, it would take years, perhaps decades, to explore the depths to any level of understanding.

How she wanted to delve into the library and scour the shelves for details about the cataclysm but it was too dangerous. They needed a battalion of guards to push any further than even this entryway.

Yeru had sent word to Scholar Sciona confirming that this was the library of Nenelan and that they would need more guards, excavation teams and more researchers now that it was clear that word about the library had already reached all across Tarris. But she didn't expect to hear back from her for weeks yet. The library was so far from Tansen and it took time to gather the resources needed for such a sizable site.

Suddenly Isin gasped and dropped the piece of bread she was holding. "Oh! I almost forgot. They have a gathering every night and talk about what they found *in good faith."*

"Great."

"And I said we would be there," Isin said.

Yeru almost spat out her food. "You what?"

"Everyone is in attendance! We can't very well be the only ones missing it."

She was right. Yeru blew out a breath.

"Plus, we can pry and see who might be members of this cult Sciona warned us about," Isin said.

Later that day the scholars slowly started drifting towards the fire in the entry chamber, outside the main library. They sat huddled together in groups. And several of the scholars were cooking in a large pot atop the curling flames of a fire pit.

A Tarrisian stew, Yeru noted. It was common in the outer villages to have a meal as a community and each family brought an ingredient to share. A man dropped in chunks of a root vegetable, followed by an older woman who brushed in a red spiced powder.

There was a secretive air as colleagues whispered to one another their findings. This contrasted the loud banter between groups at the fringes of their bubbles where they chatted about how incredible the library was but with few specifics on why.

Were all new sites like this? Yeru wondered.

Etan waved them over from across the chamber but Yeru pretended not to see and sat with Isin far from him and his group. Servants passed around bowls of the stew and the groups began to blend together like the ingredients of the meal.

Isin laughed and chatted with some scholars from a small village outside of Yontar. Yeru watched as she giggled and nudged into one of them like they were best friends. How did she do that? The ease at which they all chatted came so naturally to Isin.

And so quickly too, Yeru thought. She found it hard to be herself around new people. It took time to feel comfortable and let down the mask of social expectation.

Yeru shook her head and glanced down at her stew. Her father had always been good in these types of situations, too. He would have befriended them all and found out exactly what they had found in the library so far by now. Yeru ran the spoon through the burnt-orange stew imagining him on some ship sailing across the seas. And here she was, out of her depth at a simple gathering.

"I wouldn't eat that," Etan said.

With a swish of his scholar's robes, Etan dropped down beside her.

"And why is that?" Yeru asked.

He smiled then. An infuriatingly smug expression. "You always get so defensive."

"You just told me not to eat my stew."

Etan weighed her up as the smile faded. "I'm surprised to find you at a site. You always seemed like a…" He waved his arms around, looking for the word.

"Homebody?"

The smile returned. "Exactly."

Yeru shrugged as she glanced at the other scholars in the chamber. "Sometimes you need to see what it is you're writing about. Breathe the air that they breathed. Hear what they heard."

"Sage words. Here was me thinking that you came for the glory of discovery."

She rolled her eyes. "Is that all you think about?"

Etan's face grew hard as he stared off into the crowd. "No. But a lot of others do."

Yeru followed his gaze and it landed on the white-haired woman who had spoken to Yeru when she first arrived at the library. Whute, that was her name.

"Do you know her?" Yeru asked. "I haven't seen her before."

Etan nodded and stayed silent.

"Well? Who is she?"

"Whute is from Rizu too. A private research team."

Yeru raised an eyebrow. "And that's it?"

He glanced around before edging closer to Yeru. "What did she say to you when you arrived?"

"Nothing. Why?"

"She's dangerous, Yeru. I don't know how or why but something is off about her."

Yeru's stomach fluttered. Was she part of the cult Sciona warned her about? Whute sat in a large circle with a blend of scholars. Her shining white hair fell around a steaming cup that she pressed against her chest. There was something familiar about her.

"Does she have a team?" Yeru asked, now wary of the crowd around them.

"Yeah," Etan said. One by one he pointed out a team of around ten scholars and assistants. There was nothing remarkable about the others and Yeru didn't feel that familiarity with them like she did with Whute.

"They're very spread out," Yeru said. Few of their team sat together and instead seemed to be spaced out into every group.

"Perhaps they're trying to figure out what the other scholars have learnt so far," Etan whispered.

Yeru eyed the nearest, who was sat beside Isin. He too held a mug close to his chest like he was cold.

"What is it?" Etan asked.

"Are you cold?" Yeru asked.

Etan stared at her like she had spat on his research papers.

"He and Whute are clasping steaming mug closely, that's all." Yeru then realised that everyone in their group was holding mugs to their chest, steam drifting up to their face.

Suddenly, Yeru felt very cold. Her eyes grew wide as she spun towards the stew. The sour aroma filled the cavern. She felt a roiling in her stomach as the cavern began to spin.

"Yeru?" Etan asked.

"They're using the stew." Yeru's words seemed to

fill her mouth and she struggled to force them out. On the far side of the chamber one of the scholars toppled over. Others ran to his side when another person dropped to the ground.

"There's something in the stew," Yeru said dragging herself to her feet. "It's in the air too." Luckily she hadn't eaten any of her stew yet.

Etan said something but it was lost to the haze. She had to get out of this chamber. Now.

The doors to the library were open. Yeru stumbled over to Isin who swayed as she watched the chaos erupt around the cave. More scholars collapsed and keeled over causing confused panic.

"Yeru? What's happening?" Isin's voice was light as Yeru hauled her up. She was weak on her feet.

"Did you eat any of the stew?" Yeru snapped.

Isin's eyes were rolling. "A little. Why?"

"Come on!" Yeru pulled Isin through the chamber and towards the library. Around them, scholars were passing out and wobbling on their feet. The guard's from Whute's crew unsheathed swords to fight those who were still steady.

Etan appeared at their side. "What happened to her?" he asked grabbing Isin's other arm.

"She ate the stew," Yeru said and he grimaced.

They walked down the short corridor into the library and the sounds of fighting quietened. It was easier to breathe after they passed into the camp where the tents were set up.

Yeru eased Isin down against the balustrade, dizzying as she looked past her friend at the long drop of darkened floor after floor. Etan steadied her. "Did you eat some?" he asked.

"No, no." She clutched her head. "The fumes got to me."

The room steadied again and she felt Isin's forehead. She was burning up.

"We need to bring down her temperature," Yeru

said.

Etan ran off and came back with a wet cloth. Yeru nodded her thanks as she placed it on Isin's brow.

"We need to move. They will check in here for stragglers," Etan said as he looked around.

Yeru's thoughts were hazy but there was a lucidity to Etan. That was when she saw it. The same mug of tea that the scholars had held was in his free hand. The library spun and Yeru toppled against the railing. Etan reached out but she battered the hand away.

"What is—" Etan started but then noticed Yeru looking at the mug. "Look, Yeru. It's not what you think."

She was so dumb. Of course he was a part of this. He had warned her not to eat the stew as he sat beside her. Anger bubbled up as a hot nauseous wave. Yeru had to get Isin away from him.

Then guards rushed into the library.

The stomp of heavy boots were like impacts in Yeru's head. Two men in thick leather jerkins appeared from the corridor.

"I've got these two," Etan said.

The guards had their swords in their hands. "Do you have a weapon?" one asked as he stepped closer.

"No but I won't need one. They've both been affected," Etan said. Yeru couldn't decide if it was the disgust that brought bile up her throat or the fumes from the stew as she turned and threw up, splattering Etan's boots.

"We'll take care of them then," one of the guards said.

Etan stood. "Take care? No one is to die."

"The plans changed." The closest guard levelled his sword at Etan. "Now move."

Etan glanced over his shoulder at Yeru and fear reflected in his eyes. That same terror froze over Yeru's anger. She was in no state to fight back. She wasn't even sure if she could unfasten the dagger on her belt.

Then Etan turned and lunged.

Surprise let him pass the blade and crack the man across the nose. Blood spurted as he stumbled back dropping his sword to clutch at his face. Etan deftly grabbed the sword and brought it up, pommel hitting the man's jaw.

The first guard fell as the other swooped in with a cry. Etan dove out the way but the guard's sword caught his calf and he hissed. They traded blows. Steel against steel.

Yeru's vision swam and they became little more than clashing blurs. She focused on Isin who was breathing heavily. A thought forced itself through the mud-like pool of her mind. The tonic. Her father had always said to carry a tonic. He swore that it was the number one item that he had used on his travels. The tonic made one throw their guts up and got rid of whatever they had eaten. He said he had avoided poisons, both purposeful and accidental from off meat or foods that didn't agree with him. And she had carried one whenever she left Tansen ever since.

Yeru reached for her belt, her fingers not doing what she asked of them, fumbled for the buckles. Eventually she pulled the vial out and unstoppered it.

"Isin you have to drink this," Yeru said. Her friend didn't respond as Yeru tipped the liquid into her mouth. Isin's face tightened but she swallowed.

A scream tore her gaze back to the fight. Etan was pressed against the railing, his sword lost in the fight, as the guard pushed him closer to the edge.

He was going to fall.

Yeru spotted Etan's sword lying by their feet. She rolled over and heaved herself up. Unsteadily, Yeru trudged towards them picking up the sword as she passed. She lifted the heavy blade above her head to slice down on the guard and Etan stilled.

The guard must have sensed the change in Etan and shoved him over the railing. Yeru brought the sword down as the guard spun. He cried out as it bit into his bicep. The guard shifted and the weight of the blade carried it down and across his stomach. He stared at the gaping wound as blood began to pour onto the floor. Shock drained the blood from his face and he fell to his knees.

Yeru stared at the wound. She had done that. Hot white shock stealing all thought.

"Yeru!"

Etan was hanging onto the railing.

More guards piled down the corridor into the library.

Yeru watched as sweat made Etan's fingers glide on the stone edge. She dove grabbing his hand, but the fumes had messed with her balance and she put too much weight forward. Their hands touched as she toppled over and together they fell into the library.

5

Into the Depths

"I wonder sometimes about the importance of my work. Does this finding truly matter? Will deciphering this ancient text be useful? In the end, only time will tell."
- Yeru's Journal, page 2.

The floors passed in a blur. Yeru's stomach was in her throat, and at some point, she had let go of Etan. All she could hear was her blood pumping through her ears and the whistle of the air as they dropped into the abyss.

Then there was another noise. A high-pitched beep with a flash of light coming from one of the floors. Then it happened again on another floor as they fell past.

Then another.

And another.

Then suddenly every floor they passed flashed a light and beeped as they dropped.

There was a puff of air and a net shot out under them. It wrapped around Yeru and Etan, holding them suspended in the air, the sudden stop making Yeru's already upset stomach jerk downward.

Yeru blinked. Through the netting was the black endless drop into eternity.

Snap.

The net swung past the railing of the floor they had stopped at and spat them out onto the ground. Yeru groaned as she righted herself. Still feeling groggy from the fumes of the stew, she pulled herself up and glanced around. The net that had caught them was pulled back and sucked into a tube and out of sight. Part of her was fascinated by the device but she felt too sick to think on it.

Etan hissed as he rolled over, holding his shoulder.

Yeru couldn't believe it. They were alive. Then she turned and threw up.

It took over an hour for the effects of the fumes to wear off. In that time Yeru leant against a pillar and tried not to think. Whenever she did, her heart rate sped up and she felt her pulse in her temple.

Etan wandered off and Yeru was grateful. She didn't want to talk with him either.

I hope Isin is okay, she thought. The tonic would have her throwing her guts up by now. *As long as they are still intact to throw up.* That made her feel nauseous. She had to be okay. Yeru had to believe that Isin was okay.

After a while, Etan reappeared from between some bookshelves carrying a waterskin. He handed it to Yeru without a word. Where he had gotten the water from, Yeru wasn't sure but it tasted fresh and helped settle her stomach.

"I can't see a staircase back up. We will have to delve deeper into the library to find one," Etan said.

Yeru peered through the railing at the endless floors below and above. They should have been dead. They should have found the unseen bottom of the lost library the hard way. However the ancients must have realised the risk and created that contraption to catch any who may have fallen over the balustrade. It was ingenious. She couldn't begin to think of the mechanisms in play to track the velocity of their fall and then catch them with the net.

Yeru hauled herself up and the room only spun a little. Etan held out a hand to help but she ignored him, instead using the railing to get her feet under her. Yeru glanced upward and all she could see was floors of bookshelves with no hint of the entry chamber. It was impossible to know how far they had fallen. Light was sporadic with some floors in complete darkness. While others were lit by those strange pale light orbs.

Moss grew in patches on the floor between thin reeds rising to their knees and vines crawled up the high bookshelves that surrounded them. And in the distance, she could hear… was that running water? Was that where Etan found the waterskin? She hoped not.

It was like nature had claimed this part of the library.

She hated to agree with Etan but they did need to find a staircase and start making their way back up. Given how far they had fallen it could take some time to climb back up to the entry chamber. Yeru pushed off the railing and headed towards the shelves, careful to step around the thicker patches of plant life.

"So what you're just going to ignore me?" Etan said.

She walked down one of the aisles of shelves and studied the spines. Miraculously despite the moss and vines and the strange ecosystem brewing down here, the books were undamaged and untouched by growth or mould. How could that be? Some ancient deterrent that they didn't know about? Yeru inspected the books but she couldn't see anything that would stop the flora from spreading onto the tomes.

Part of her was in awe of the library but a louder, more present part screamed at her about the potential dangers. They could not protect themselves from what they did not understand and right now they were in the belly of an unknown beast.

"Yeru, come on."

Yeru spun to face Etan.

"It's not what it looks like," he said.

"Not what it looks like? So you aren't working with Whute? So you weren't part of *that*?" Yeru waved her hands upward searching for the right words to describe what had happened.

"Are they dead, Etan?" Her voice was cold and emotionless. She hadn't let herself think about it until now but everyone in that chamber might be dead. It should have been a startling revelation but there was no flare of anger or grief or panic. Instead, a cold wave of resignation washed over her and dragged her down into the depths of unfeeling.

"No, Yeru. I…" Etan rubbed his face and sighed. "I don't know. This wasn't what was supposed to happen."

"Well what was supposed to happen?" Yeru snapped as she marched towards him, finger pointed. Her blood thrummed as the rage finally boiled up. "You had one of those mugs too, to stop the scent. You saw what Whute and the guards did. What conclusion am I supposed to make?"

Etan opened his mouth to respond.

Slam.

They silenced and heads spun to face where the sound had emanated from. Etan was about to speak when Yeru brought a finger to her lips to silence him, and then together they crept towards the edge of the bookshelves. Yeru peeked around to see an open space. It had once been a reading area with many chairs spread around small circular tables backed by ceiling to floor bookshelves. Now it closer resembled an overgrown ruin. Greenery sprouted up the side of the shelves and covered the sandstone floor.

Huge leaves shifted in the brush. Then a nose poked out. It was a black short snout. It wiggled, sniffing the air before the creature pushed past the leaf. It was no larger than Yeru's forearm with a long brown furred body and ferret-like face. Its tail was thin with a leaf shaped tip. The creature froze when it spotted Yeru and Etan and hopped onto its back legs. Its small arm reached back and scratched behind its ear.

"What is—" Etan's voice startled the beast and it dove back into the brush and disappeared.

Yeru blew out a breath and stepped out from behind the bookshelf. "That was a leaf-tipped feran."

Etan raised an eyebrow. "Feran? Aren't they—"

"Extinct. Yes." Yeru wandered through the ankle-high grass and ran her hand over the leaves. "Or so we thought. I remember reading about a case where a traveller saw one near Asuriya two hundred years ago but there have been no sightings since."

How a feran had survived this deep in the library, Yeru wasn't sure. It would need food, mates, and clean water to survive. She had read about enclosed ecosystems found deep underground, where scholars discovered new and old species. But this was a *library*. Yeru had expected to find books and a place of learning. Not a dead species walking its corridors.

"We're going to have to be careful," Yeru said. "If a feran is down here, who knows what else could have survived."

"Yeru."

She glanced up to see Etan staring at something past the bookshelves. As she approached, the sound of running water got louder. Around the corner past the next line of bookshelves was a fountain. Clear flowing water spat out of a statue of a deity Yeru didn't recognise. It was shaped like a serpent coiling upward. The water dropped down into the pool around its base where four other ferans floundered about. Yeru stared in awe as they dove under the water and came up with a splash.

"They're playing," Etan said.

A moment later one of the ferans went rigid as it saw them. It squeaked and the ferans fled from the fountain into the nearby shelving.

"This is insane," Etan said.

Slowly they made their way into the reading area. Yeru dipped her hand in the water. It was clear. "Is this where you filled up my waterskin?"

He nodded with a grimace. "But I took it from the running water at the top, not the pool. I'm not a fool, Yeru. Besides, I read that they had drinking fountains in the library for those who were reading, so it should be fresh."

Yeru was about to tip out the rest of her waterskin then she hesitated. They had no idea how long it would take to find a way out. And it *had* tasted fresh. She stoppered the top of the waterskin and tied it back onto her belt.

"Fill up yours." Yeru gestured to the fountain.

As Etan clambered onto the edge of the pool, Yeru wandered around the open seating area.

"No one was supposed to die, Yeru," Etan said as he leant against the statue and filled his waterskin. She continued to walk by the bookshelves. "I got a letter from the monarch of Rizu that night at the Cartographer's Rest inn. It said that my team was to stand back and let Whute knock you all out. It was supposed to be quick so that we could have extra time to lay claim to the discovery. I swear they didn't say anything about anyone getting hurt. Yeru you have to believe me."

Yeru searched his face for a hint of a lie. A betraying twitch. A nervous glance away. She found none, and yet did she really know this man? Clearly not as well as she thought.

"The monarch of Rizu?" Yeru asked.

Etan nodded. "That's why I trusted it. I didn't think they would..." His voice trailed off.

Scholar Sciona would want to know about this. Was Whute part of this cult she had warned Yeru about? Was Etan?

She bit the inside of her lip. If he was, he would have likely tried to kill her while she was incapacitated. But perhaps he knew that they would need each other if they were to find their way out of the library. He *had* protected Yeru and Isin from the guards, too.

"Let's just focus on getting out of here," she said.

Creatures scuttled through the book stacks and underbrush as Yeru and Etan made their way through the library. Books lay strewn across the floor, loose pages scattered around them. Tables had been toppled and chairs tossed aside, whether from animals or the humans from when the library was open Yeru could not tell. After an inspection of claw marks that had splintered one of the bookshelves they decided to quickly move on.

Yeru bent down and picked up a page. It was about farming. Most of the books she had checked so far were about agriculture in some form or another. Some of it surprised Yeru. Books this old shouldn't have held the level of information that they did. They contained more advanced techniques than she thought possible for the age. There was a popular modern day theory about Tarrisians losing knowledge after the cataclysm that destroyed their old capital and this seemed to further confirm those suspicions.

They reached a wide walkway with a plush red carpet running down the centre, lined with bookshelves on either side. The ceiling rose to four storeys in height.

"A directory!" Etan said and jogged over to a meaty tome sat atop a pedestal. Tall grass surrounded the elevated platform in the middle of the red carpet. He leafed through the pages as Yeru approached. "Here." He pointed to one of the first pages which contained a map. It depicted a grid-like system of bookshelves with open seating areas placed throughout. There were some larger openings than those they had come across so far and an area that looked to be made up of booths and reading nooks. Breaking up this section of the library was the red line mirroring the carpet at their feet. It ran through the middle of this *'Agriculture at Altitude'* wing of the floor and led all the way to a stair symbol.

"If we follow this, I think we'll reach the staircase," Etan said.

Yeru slid out a blank scroll and started to sketch part of the map.

"What're you doing?" Etan asked.

"That tome is far too large to bring with us. So I'm making a basic copy of the map," she said scratching the long straight onto the page. Etan grunted his ascent and moved to the side so that she could get a better view. Etan hopped off the platform.

Crunch.

He let out a cry and jumped to the side. "What was that?" he hissed. Etan brushed the high grass aside and saw that he had stomped on something ashen. He reached down and pulled up a shard. The second it was revealed, Etan squealed and threw the piece away. It was a skull. Or at least part of one. Yeru carefully stepped down into the grass and together they dropped to their haunches to inspect the bones.

"There's enough bones here for at least two people," Yeru said nudging the bones with her foot.

"But only one skull," Etan noted. He left the question of the missing skull between them.

"You know. We've never asked why the library went missing in the first place. It moves. That much is clear but why was it left? Was it abandoned?" Yeru asked.

"Or fled from," Etan said and met her gaze.

"Let's keep moving," Yeru said.

Despite the quiet of the library, they moved in silence down the red carpet overgrown with knee high grass and shrubbery around the edges of the shelves.

It had been Isin who noticed the strange lack of sound within the library. Yeru often shut off the outside world so that she could focus, so it was only when Isin explained to her that the library was too quiet that she realised what Isin meant. No one knew how it worked but sound didn't travel as far in the library. Yeru could see why this would be helpful for those needing silence to think when the library had been full of people, but in this dead place it held an eerie atmosphere.

Insects crept up the vines as they passed. Unseen animals shook the far off plants but few came close enough to see.

Eventually the staircase came into view. As they came closer, the grand scale of the steps became more apparent. Yeru's mouth fell open in awe at the size of the staircase. The opening was two storeys tall. Light orbs were placed up the sides of the wall bathing the perfectly cut stone with pale light.

Etan let out a laugh of relief. "We made it."

There was movement at the corner of Yeru's eye.

She spun but only the expansive library was at their backs.

"What is it?" Etan asked.

"I thought I saw something," she said peering into the grass. Everything was still.

"Probably another walking extinct species but let's not wait and find out." Etan laid a hand on Yeru's shoulder. She shook it off and scowled at him. Then she pushed past and ascended the stairs.

6

What Separates Us

"Often the histories are seen as pieces of a puzzle to be fit together. But sometimes we need to remember that they are fragments of a whole. And not all pieces are always account for."

- Yeru's Journal, page 78.

Yeru was glad to be off the floor and moving upward. Light orbs lit the way as they climbed three floors in silence inspecting the incredible marvel of architecture. *The steps are so smooth,* Yeru thought in wonder. They had no seams or edges as if the staircase had been cut into the stone itself.

"Let me talk with Whute when we get up there. I'm sure we can add another name to the discovery once I explain everything," Etan said.

Yeru rounded on him. "What are you talking about?"

"The discovery of the library?"

"They killed people, Etan! I have no interest in being

part of this," she said. How could he still care about the accolades when their colleagues were being murdered?

He screwed his face up as if he hadn't expected this response. "I know that. I'll bring it up with the scholars when I return to Rizu, but Yeru." He came to her side and took her hands. "They will claim this discovery no matter what. I don't agree with them but once we get up there, we don't have another choice. Can't you see that? They'll kill us if we challenge them."

Yeru scoffed and threw his hands off. "We need to fight back. This isn't about the library anymore. They are killing our people. And well…" She wasn't supposed to tell anyone this but she had to get Etan on her side for what was to come. "There is a cult. One that follows a deity called Ma-lin."

"The deity of lies?" He raised one eyebrow. Yeru gauged his reaction hoping to catch a tick that might imply he was part of the cult but he looked genuinely surprised. If he knew of the deity and cult, Etan did a good job hiding it.

Yeru nodded. "The cult is said to believe that the cataclysm was an event used to hide knowledge we cannot be trusted with. And they sabotage research trying to uncover our past all the time."

"And you think Whute is part of this cult?"

"It would make sense."

Blowing out a breath, Etan ran a hand through his hair. "If that is true then that is more reason to follow along. They must have connections in the monarchy to have come this far."

"No, it's more reason to push against them! They might kill us anyway," Yeru said.

"Yeru, look—" Etan glanced up at her and then past her shoulder and his face tightened.

"What?" Yeru asked as she followed his gaze. On the next landing between the staircases there was a huge rock. The stairwell had been clear up until this point.

The next staircase had collapsed in on itself with

chunks of stone scattered across the landing. Etan hopped onto a boulder and pulled at the pile of rocks but they wouldn't budge.

"Sands suffocate us. We aren't going to be able to get through this," Etan said.

Yeru slid the notebook out of her belt and opened to the map. "If all the floors match then there should be another staircase on the opposite side."

"How far is that?" Etan asked.

Yeru shrugged. "There was no scale indication. I think the map was only for that local chamber of shelves and reading areas on agriculture. Who knows how many of these wings there are on each floor."

"We better get moving then," he said with a sigh.

As they made their way back down to the nearest floor, Yeru slowed. A deep thrumming reverberated from further down the stairwell.

"What is it?" Etan asked. She hushed him. There it was again.

And it was getting louder.

"Yeru—"

"Shh!"

Etan furrowed his brow and was about to say something else when Yeru gestured for him to listen. They stood ears perked and coming from the staircase below was the unmistakable sound of footsteps.

Something was following them.

Etan's eyes widened as he heard it too.

"Move," Yeru hissed.

They rushed down to the landing below and out into the floor proper. Behind, claws scratched against stone. The strange sound dampening in the library made it hard to judge the distances of sounds, but if they could hear the scraping of claws and impact of footsteps, then whatever was following them was sure to be near.

The floor was darker than the others they had passed but they took no time to survey it. There was no time. They shot out into the shelves that rose all the way to the high ceiling. Much of what was around them was shrouded in darkness and impossible to see. Yeru hoped that meant whatever was on their heels would struggle to see them as much as they would it.

"Yeru, over here," Etan said as he ran for one of the bookshelves. It had a ladder attached that led up to a balcony walkway that covered the bookshelf allowing easier access to the higher shelves. Etan clambered up and Yeru launched herself after him. Vines wrapped around the cold metal. Upon making it onto the walkway, they lay flat and stared at the entrance to the floor.

Thud.

Thud.

Thud.

The creature was at least a storey tall. Bile rose up Yeru's throat at the sight of the beast. Each plodding footstep showed the creature's contracting and stretching muscles. Its torso took up most of its height and it was a mess of organs pumping and nerves twitching. Even with the little light there was, Yeru saw that the creature's thin skin was ashen, its face a bedraggled mess of wiry hair. The sunken eye sockets only hinted at the eyes within.

Yeru hadn't heard of anything like it. Her brain scrambled to find some comparison to a creature of the past but she came up short.

It stopped. The creature's head swivelled back and forth. Yeru felt like her body would convulse if her heart beat any harder. A tremor wound its way through her body. It was like something out of a nightmare. No creature like this could exist outside of the page.

It tilted its head up and the flab of meat upon its face twitched. It was sniffing the air, Yeru realised.

The beast's head moved towards them.

"We need to go," Yeru whispered.

Etan was staring wide eyed and unmoving, enraptured by the horror of the creature.

"Etan." Yeru poked him and he shook himself out his stupor. He nodded and together they crawled along the walkway. Yeru held her breath trying not to make a sound as they inched away from the creature. It seemed to have caught onto their scent and moved in their direction. The creature's head was taller than the walkway. If it got close enough it would see them.

It marched through the library.

"Faster," Yeru said. They hopped up onto their haunches, Yeru hoping the low light was enough to mask their shapes as they darted across the walkway.

They got to the end of the shelves where a railing led onto a ladder dropping back down to ground level.

"Damn it," Etan said. The creature would be upon them by the time they reached the bottom. Not to mention that going back to ground level was a death sentence.

"The vines!" Yeru said, pointing. Vines sprouted along the shelves in a web of greenery.

Etan clambered out onto the end of the bookshelf, using the vines as a handhold. Yeru glanced over her shoulder and the thing was getting closer. Those black sockets drew her in until the library around her fell away. The muscles around its face pulsed and twitched and its thudding footsteps rang through her head like the toll of death's bell.

"Yeru!"

She gasped coming back from her reprieve and dove out onto the bookshelves. They clambered along quickly but it was hard going. Yeru grabbed a vine and it ripped from the roots, unable to hold her weight. Her heart shot up her throat as she caught another cord that held. She tested each vine giving it a yank before using it to move along the shelf.

The creature continued to plod after them. Yeru didn't think the beast saw them yet so it had to be following their scent.

"Scent," Yeru said.

"What?"

"We need to mask our scent," Yeru said.

Etan froze and nodded in understanding. They started ripping out vines and books and rubbing them against their skin and clothing. If only they had dunked themselves in that fountain.

The sucking of air sounded like wind being pulled through a tunnel, and Yeru glanced up to see the creature staring at them.

It stopped moving.

"Maybe it can't see," Etan whispered.

The creature howled. It was like the calls of many men dying. And then it broke into a run. It was faster than what should have been possible for its huge size.

"Jump!" Etan screamed. Yeru leapt from the bookshelf.

The beast crashed into the bookshelf sending books and dust pluming outward. Yeru fell through the cloud of dust and burst through a stack of books. She rolled, coughing and spluttering. Blinking the dust from her eyes, Yeru peered into the black. It was too dark to see much in this part of the library but it was clear that some books had broken her fall.

"Etan?" she whispered.

There was movement in the dark. "I'm here."

The beast hissed, shook its head and righted itself. Then it turned its nose upward. Yeru's blood ran cold. It would find them here and they couldn't flee in this darkness.

"The books," Etan said. "Get under the books!"

To hide their scent, Yeru realised, and started burying herself under the tomes that lay around her. Burrowing herself into a pile that completely covered her body Yeru stilled, breathing hard.

The footsteps stopped.

The harsh inhale of sniffing.

Yeru forced her eyes shut as a tear ran down her

cheek. It was right there. If it picked up on her scent she was dead. The creak of books being walked on told her the creature was moving again.

Suddenly the pile of books Yeru was under shifted and they dropped away revealing the faint far off light from the entrance to the floor. Yeru stifled a yelp as she saw the darkened form of the creature above.

Clawing her way back under the books, Yeru swallowed back the bile rising up her throat. Its head rotated and the neck muscles glistened in the low light. It stayed like that for some time. Nose lifted high and unmoving. Finally it groaned, turned and then stomped further into the library.

Yeru waited until it was out of sight before letting out a quiet cry. Etan appeared at her side and sat back against the books, clutching at his chest.

"What was that?" he asked, his voice shaking.

Yeru rubbed at her arms. "I don't know. I... We can't stay here."

They made their way back towards the light of the entrance keeping to the edges of the shelves. All around, the darkness spread like smog. Why was it so dark on this floor?

"Should we go down?" Etan asked.

With the way up blocked they had no way to continue their ascent but Yeru couldn't face going deeper into the library either. She shook her head. "That thing came from further down. More stairwells could be blocked. We should remain as high as we can and search for more staircases."

"The floor below is lit," Etan said.

He was right. She remembered peering out into the well-lit stacks. Part of her wanted nothing more than to return to the light but that was her animal mind talking. Her father's words echoed in her head.

'When all goes wrong we return to our base instincts. Fear freezes and reverts us to nothing more than a beast. That is when we must do better. That is when we must

remember what separates us from the wild creatures of the world.'

"We shouldn't go deeper just for some light. The dark will help hide us. And besides," Yeru pulled one of the working light orbs from its fixtures. The head sized orb felt like glass in her hands as she rolled it between her palms. "We can use these."

Etan didn't seem so sure.

"Look," Yeru said. There was still a tremor in her voice. "The other scholars talked about contained ecosystems and the risks they bring. Yes we may find extinct creatures we know of, but there are likely many we don't know as well. The lower we go, the more we risk running into those things.

"That monster saw us. We can use the dark to cross the floor to the other side and the staircases there," Yeru said. She still couldn't shake those darkened eye sockets staring at her. A shiver ran down her back.

"Across the entire floor?"

Yeru nodded. Etan sighed but he knew it was the only way. Etan reached over and grabbed an orb of his own and together they trekked out into the darkness.

7

The Masks of Ma-nivi

"The difference between a historian and a dreamer is that historians know that people from all ages lie."
                    - Yeru's Journal, page 134.

Yeru pushed back the darkness with the light of the thrumming orb within her hand. As she walked, Yeru inspected the orb but saw no seams or seals. And yet, it was too round to be natural.

"Do you think these run on a fuel source?" Yeru whispered. The library suppressed sound but after their run in at the stairwell she couldn't bring herself to speak up.

Etan grunted lifting his orb up. "I have no idea. If they do, they have an incredibly long life," he said. "Thousands of years these have been lit under here."

"Perhaps this floor is one of the first to run out of whatever fuel source these use and that's why it's so dark compared to the other floors," Yeru said. If the ancients refilled or exchanged the light orbs on a floor by floor basis, it made sense that they would fade at the same time.

The floor was much like the one they had landed on, with floor to ceiling bookshelves. Some areas were open to create spaces for reading with benches and fountains for drinking. At the first fountain, they wet their skin to further mask their scent. Hopefully it would be enough.

Books lay shredded at the base of the shelves and stacks were toppled into mounds. Yeru guessed there had been some kind of altercation on this floor from the creatures living here. Sadly this meant that they found no directory that would have contained a map.

Hints of life lay scattered among the stacks of books. Shrubbery shifted upon their passing. Nest-like burrow openings had been dug into the bookshelves. And Yeru caught sight of several small animals fleeing from their light.

Etan spotted movement first.

Something as large as a kiren, coming up to Yeru's shoulder, walking on all fours. They slid their orbs beneath their cloaks and ducked into one of the aisles.

The beast sauntered past without a glance in their direction. It was cat-like aside from its size. The brown fur was patchy revealing scars that covered its flesh.

They waited long after it had gone from sight before continuing.

The library enclosed itself. What was once grand halls of shelves became smaller nooks and winding tunnel-like corridors. Yeru hoped this was a good sign and that they were reaching the far side of the floor.

"Yeru, come and have a look at this," Etan said.

Yeru turned and made her way down the branching corridor Etan had been checking. He pointed to a fixture on the wall. One that should have held the light orbs. "Have you seen one of those orbs not lit yet?" he asked.

She shook her head. Then he pointed to the ground. There scattered across the floor were shards of what looked to be glass.

"It shattered?" Yeru asked dropping to her haunches to inspect the fragments.

"Or was destroyed," Etan said.

Yeru grunted as she picked a piece up. It was sharp and bit into her skin, drawing blood. She hissed and dropped it.

"Careful," Etan said.

"Thank you for that insightful comment," she said.

Yeru stood and squinted down the corridor. "Is that a staircase?"

True enough, at the end of the corridor was a short stairwell. It wasn't the grand steps between the floors but at least they were moving in the right direction. Yeru and Etan shared a glance before smothering their orbs so that only a pale light shone through their cloaks and they climbed the steps. A long stone corridor with many doors on each side stretched out in front of them.

Coming to the first door, Yeru readied herself and then pushed it. The door swung open to a bedroom chamber. It was not the empty shell of a room that one would find at an inn but the personal quarters of someone who had lived there for a time. Yeru crept in feeling like she was intruding somewhere private. A desk sat in the far corner with a book held open by a paper weight. Etan swung open the cupboard doors and clothes still hung inside.

Wandering over to the bed, Yeru found a piece of parchment folded to resemble a sand fox sitting on the backboard of the cot.

"Someone lived here," Yeru said.

Everything was coated in a thick layer of dust showing untouched ages passed. But someone had lived in the library.

"The librarians perhaps?" Etan offered.

Yeru supposed that could be the case. She thought

of Scholar Athor in the Tansen Archive and his family outside of the library. He was always excited to finish and see his wife and kids. To live in the library would be different kind of life.

They checked the rooms one by one and found them much the same. All were living quarters with personal items. Yeru wondered again what made the Tarrisians leave the library in the first place. There were books left open and Etan had even found a half-eaten meal decomposed upon a plate as if they had left in the knowledge that they would return soon. And yet something had stopped them from coming back.

At the far side of the corridor, the stairwell led back down. Yeru grimaced. So much for moving upward.

Something caught her eye at the bottom of the stairwell.

A face.

It drew back into the dark as quickly as it had appeared.

"Hey!" Yeru said.

"What?" Etan asked coming out from the last room.

"I thought I saw… a girl," Yeru said. It had looked like a young girl but it was hard to tell in the smothering darkness.

Etan raised a sceptical eyebrow. "We've been wandering the library for too long. Maybe we should stop and rest."

"No. Come on," Yeru said and took to the steps. The more she thought about it the more she was sure about what she saw. Etan called after her but Yeru ignored him and tore down the steps. They came out in a huge chamber with rows of stalls around them like a market square. Yeru came to a halt. It wasn't just like a market square, she realised lifting up the light orb, this had once been a market.

"Yeru we can't…" his voice trailed off as he looked around the chamber coming to the same conclusion as Yeru.

The library of Nenelan had been a city.

Suddenly the contradicting reports made more sense. Some called it a place of knowledge but others, a sanctuary. Because it was all of the above.

A dark blur shot out from under one of the stalls and this time Yeru was ready. Raising the light orb, she got a better look and it was undoubtedly a young girl. She wore leathery rags and her skin was smothered in a black paint of some kind but this was no monster.

"Wait!" Yeru called.

The girl faced her wide eyed. There was fear in those eyes. And then she took off into the market square.

"That was a girl," Etan said.

"Come on."

They chased the girl as she dived over and rolled under stalls but they had no chance keeping up with the agile girl. And soon she was lost to the dark.

Yeru bent over, panting. Sweat trickled down her brow. Etan was equally out of breath leaning against one of the stalls.

"Fast little thing," he said between breaths.

Yeru lifted her orb as she regained her breath and shouted into the dark. "We don't want to hurt you!"

The black did not answer.

"If there's a girl in here, that means there must be—"

As if calling them into existence, masked people appeared from the shadows. Yeru and Etan drew together as more and more came into the light of their orbs. Their masks were in the likeness of Ma-nivi, the owl deity of knowledge. Yeru recognised it immediately.

"We mean no harm," Yeru said.

Long poles with bladed ends were levelled at Yeru and Etan and they raised their hands in surrender.

There was a howl in the distance and the masked people all spun to face the noise. They chattered amongst themselves in a language Yeru didn't recognise but the tone was urgent. Suddenly two masked figures swept in from behind and held blades to Yeru and Etan's throats.

"*Irivi*," the man whispered.

That sounded awfully like *irva*. The old tongue word for silence. Did they speak a form of the old tongue? Had these people been down here since the library was lost?

"Etan, I think—" Yeru started but the blade at her neck drew closer and again the man whispered the word.

The wail came again closer this time.

The people burst into action. Yeru was pulled down low to her haunches. Another of the masked people yanked the orb from her hands and rolled it away and they did the same with Etan's. Yeru wanted to protest but the blade already drew blood at her neck so she stayed quiet.

Then they were on the move. Yeru stumbled and was dragged under stalls and through the library. She tripped and walked into things in the dark. How the masked people could see so well in the dark, Yeru wasn't sure, but the man leading her did his best to keep her upright and moving at their pace.

They did not hear another cry from the monster in the dark.

After some time of moving, Yeru's eyes adjusted to see rough shapes. Not enough to stop herself from falling over books laying strewn on the floor but enough that she hadn't walked into any more bookshelves. Several times the party stopped. They made no movement or sound. Yeru guessed they had spotted some creature in the library that she couldn't see, but couldn't be sure.

The fourth time they stopped she heard the snapping of wood on wood and then the man pushed down on her head so that Yeru knew to duck as they crawled through a small space.

After clambering through a tunnel in the dark, the area around them opened and light was seen in the distance. There were quiet mutters among the masked people again and Yeru caught more words from their dialect. Some of it *was* like the old tongue. Enough that Yeru began to believe that it was indeed some offshoot language of the dead tongue. However, there was enough that she didn't recognise that translating the conversations was near impossible. She wondered if Etan picked up more than her.

They moved towards the light and Yeru started to see her surroundings. It was a high ceiling chamber but some of the bookshelves had been removed and instead the books were stacked like an outer wall of a city. More of those masked soldiers stood watch on the empty high shelves with bows at their side like guards at watch towers. A settlement?

Perhaps she should have feared these people more but after seeing the monsters within the library there was something calming about finding other humans.

"Their weapons are primitive," Etan said appearing at her side. Their escorts seemed to be less interested in holding them now that they were closer to their hide-out. "But the way they move speaks of some sort of training. Did you hear the tapping?"

Yeru furrowed her brow. "Tapping?"

"They tapped to each other as we moved through the library instead of talking. Some sort of code so they could stay quiet," Etan said. She had heard something but assumed it was shuffling.

They were led past the wall of books and onto a narrow path with high bookshelves on either side. Light orbs were placed regularly here. It was blinding after wandering through the dark for so long and Yeru had to squint to see. Now that they were inside the walls of the settlement, the people didn't wear the masks of Ma-nivi or have their skin painted with black marks. Curious eyes watched them as they passed.

The long straight of empty bookshelves opened up to a square where a crowd gathered around a fountain.

A woman stood in the centre of the throng, with hands on her hips watching as their party approached. She was dark of skin with a shaven head. Those in their party took their masks off and bowed to the woman.

A leader then, Yeru thought.

Then she spoke with words that Yeru did not recognise. However, she gestured to Yeru and Etan and by the tonality of her voice, Yeru guessed she was questioning the party about their unexpected guests. The man at the front of their procession spoke and the woman did not look pleased with his response.

After a few shared words she pushed through the crowd and marched up to Yeru and Etan.

"*Se na elvatu?*" she asked.

Yeru felt all the eyes of these people on her. "I'm sorry I don't understand."

The woman frowned and repeated the question. "*Se na elvatu?*"

"I don't speak your language," Yeru said.

"We're from outside of the library," Etan said.

The leader faced Etan and then spat at his feet. "*Bevi nateru.*"

Etan cleared his throat and stepped back. "Okay, I think she'd rather speak to you."

The woman squinted at Yeru. How could she explain? Yeru didn't even know if these people had ventured outside of the library before. After a tense silence the woman blew out a breath and waved her hand. Two men swept in and grabbed Yeru and Etan dragging them away from the crowd.

As they were taken away Yeru met eyes with the young girl she had seen first. Yeru smiled at the girl but she withdrew, hiding behind a woman's leg.

8

The Face of Another

"History is told by the survivors. But survivors do not see the worst the world has to offer."
                    - Yeru's Journal, page 103.

The masked people of the library had built a city. Yeru expected a ramshackle shelter made from the bookshelves of the grand chamber but these people had created an entire civilization upon the bones of the library. Floor to ceiling structures were built using the bookshelves as the foundation. Men and woman stuck their heads out of their homes using the shelves to create floors of the many buildings. Ropes were strung high above the aisle, that acted as a street, clothing hanging and drying in the cool air, which was fresh despite the densely packed homes. Yeru wondered at that and what they did with their waste.

People stopped and pointed at Yeru and Etan as they passed. Some grew pale and cowered like they had seen a black sand phantom.

"What is that all about?" Etan asked after one perturbed man slammed his door shut at the sight of them.

They came to a set of stairs at a quiet part of the city and the guards led them downward and into, what Yeru thought must have once been a reading room. It had been stripped of plush chairs and tables. Markings covered the walls. Not the art of the library or even the work of a scholar, these were the primitive scratchings of a mad man. A prison cell, Yeru guessed.

The guard gestured they step into the room and once Yeru and Etan had both entered the door crashed shut on their heels.

Etan started circling the room, checking the walls for another way out.

"To think there are people living down here," Yeru said.

Slamming his fist against the wall, Etan let out a breath. "It's sealed. One way in and out."

"What language do you suppose they speak?" Yeru asked as she pulled one of her journal scrolls from her belt and started taking notes of the words she had understood.

"I only caught words," Etan said.

"It sounded like the old tongue but different. Do you think it predates the old tongue or is an evolution of it?" Her mind whirled as she scribbled down her thoughts. This was the biggest finding… perhaps ever.

"It most likely postdates the old tongue. If these people have truly lived down here since the cataclysm their language will have evolved separate from modern day Tarrisian."

He was right. Yeru was thinking of these people as ancient but they weren't. They were a splinter of modern day Tarrisians. *They may know as little as we do about the cataclysm and ancient times,* Yeru thought.

"We need to find out a way to communicate with

them," Yeru said.

"Yeru."

"If we start with the differences in the old tongue compared to what they said, we can perhaps make guesses on some of the other changes and language rules that perhaps have—"

"Yeru."

Yeru glanced up and blinked. Etan leant against the wall. He suddenly looked tired. His posture was slumped and bags hung beneath his eyes. "We don't know anything about these people. You saw how they looked at us. They're suspicious of us. We don't know what life has been like down here."

He didn't have to mention the monsters roaming the dark of the library.

"This is about survival," Etan said.

Yeru cleared her throat. "You're right. I got carried away."

They were still trapped within the lost library of Nenelan. Seeing human faces amongst the monsters and shelves had settled some of Yeru's nerves but these weren't her people. And whether being found by them was a good thing or not was yet to be seen. She took a moment to ground herself and take in her surroundings, as her father had taught her to do when she was feeling overwhelmed.

The door.

A discarded book in the corner of the room.

Markings on the wall.

Yeru squinted. Was that the entry chamber to the library? She stepped up to the illustration and ran a finger over it. It was undoubtedly the same entrance they had entered the library through. The huge, glowing orb was portrayed in front of the grand doors and through those doors was darkness. Scribbles and lines scratched as threats around the door as if to warn of the evil past the threshold of the library.

"They're afraid." Yeru hadn't realised that she said

the words aloud until Etan responded.

"What?"

"Look," she said gesturing to the wall. "Think about it. If these people have been here since the cataclysm, perhaps they sheltered in here after the fallout. We know that the immediate effects must have been catastrophic. It still affects our wildlife around Asuriya today.

"Imagine thousands of years and generations speaking only of the dangers and why they fled deep into the library. Of course they would see the outside as a threat. It's likely they haven't seen another human that wasn't born in this settlement and that's why they're so cautious of us."

Etan was nodding. "That makes sense. We can use this. Explain that the outside isn't what they think it is."

"They aren't going to believe us. We're strangers and this is how the world works in their eyes. But we can show them," Yeru said.

Etan raised an eyebrow. He opened his mouth to speak when the door to their chamber creaked and swung open.

An elderly man walked in and the door snapped shut behind him. He was alone without guards. He stared at them and sucked on his gums before smacking his lips. Readjusting his gaudy green and yellow robes, he walked towards them.

"*Hevna erbalu?*" he asked.

"Great, here we go again," Etan said.

"I don't understand," Yeru said in the old tongue.

"You speak dead words," the man said in the old tongue.

Yeru and Etan glanced at one another. "You speak the old tongue?" she asked.

He sniffed and sat down on the step coming down from the door. "Most of the books in this library are written in it."

"You have to help us." Yeru rushed towards him. "We fell into the library but we're from outside."

As she approached, the man not so subtly rested his hand on the dagger at his waist and Yeru slowed.

"Are you a nightwalker?" he asked.

Nightwalker. Yeru hadn't heard the word before and so looked to Etan but he was equally perplexed.

"What is a nightwalker?" Etan asked.

In a swish faster than Yeru's eyes could track, the man pulled the dagger from the scabbard. Fire ran up the blade in a rush of light and heat. Yeru and Etan jumped back with a yelp as he waved it before them.

Yeru thought the man might have had a legendary diera blade but after seeing some sort of alchemical liquid drip off the dagger she decided that this must be some chemical reaction.

"Do you wear the skin of one of us? The face of another?" the man shouted as he moved towards them flicking the blade back and forth in a warding motion.

"No! We're human!" Etan shouted back.

"Prove it!"

"How?" Yeru asked.

"Bleed." The man spat the word and for a second Yeru thought he might stab one of them but instead, he waited.

Understanding blossomed and Etan stepped forward and held his hand out, palm up. The man carefully drew a line with the blade upon his palm and a thin line of blood welled. Etan hissed and pulled away his hand. Pained by the flames as much as the cut, Yeru guessed.

The man peered closely as blood dripped to the floor. Then he nodded and slid the dagger back into its sheathe.

"We are sorry for such precautions but it has been many generations since we've been in contact with any other tribes. We had to be sure," he said.

Tribes? Yeru's eyes widened. "There are other

groups of people in the library?"

The elderly man raised an eyebrow.

"As we said, we're from outside," Etan said clasping his hands together to stop the bleeding.

"What kind of trickery is this?" the man asked.

Yeru raised her hands. "No tricks. It's true. We fell from the entry chamber."

"You're from the higher levels?" he asked.

"No, you damn fool," Etan said. "Outside!"

Yeru scowled at Etan. She could tell the cut and conversation was grating on him but that was no way to speak to those holding them captive.

"That is impossible." The man spoke as if the words were as irrefutable as the stone around them.

"It's true," Yeru murmured and stepped towards the man. "Can you help us get back to the entry chamber? We can show you."

She could tell that the old man didn't believe what they had said but there was a curiosity in his eyes. He sniffed. "I will speak to the *artuke*."

Yeru didn't recognise the last word but guessed he meant their leader. Perhaps there wasn't a translation in the old tongue for the term. She nodded gratefully and the man retreated out of the reading room.

After he left, Yeru turned to Etan. "How is your hand?"

"I'll live." He clutched his arm to his chest and sighed. "Do you think they'll let us go?"

"I don't know." Her words echoed around the chamber.

It was some time before anyone returned. However, it gave Yeru time to think. Her father always said you can solve any problem if you had the time to figure it out. And yet this was a puzzle that mere hours wouldn't untangle.

After hours of staring at the same walls the door ground open and two guards marched in and grabbed

Yeru and Etan. Once again they were dragged through the streets. This time they were pulled onto what seemed to be a main thoroughfare.

Light orbs lit the wide open walkway between shelves that had been repurposed into buildings. It was busier than when they had entered the city, with men and woman and children wandering the street. At the end of the straight was a wall that rose two thirds of the way to the high ceiling. A single small opening was the only way through. It was covered by a tarp with two guards standing on either side.

After a quick word with the guards, Yeru and Etan were led through.

Yeru's eyes widened. On the far side of the wall were the steps leading up to the next floor. The grand archway framed the stairwell that rose up to the landing where a massive blockade had been erected. And in front of that blockade was a throne.

The dark-skinned bald woman they had met at the entrance to the settlement sat upon the brass throne. Pieces of metal stuck out from a circular back mimicking the icon for Ova's great Sun Eye. A group of five men and five woman sat on the steps leading up to the throne and they all watched in silence. Yeru recognised one as the elderly man who had come to their chamber and cut Etan. He made no sign of welcome as Yeru and Etan approached.

Tense silence filled the space and neither party broke the quiet until one of the men on the steps cleared his throat.

"You speak the ancient words?" the woman on the throne asked. The elderly man must have told her that Yeru and Etan could understand the old tongue. Etan nodded.

"This is well. I am Ikam, leader of the one hundred and twenty third floor," Ikam said. Yeru's eyes bulged. They had fallen one hundred and twenty three floors? Her mind whirled. She knew it must have been far but one hundred and twenty three?

"From what floor have you come?" Ikam asked.

Etan took a step forward. "We're from outside of the library."

This caused a stir in the ten people sat on the steps. Ikam rapped her knuckles on the throne and they fell silent. "This is impossible. None can survive outside."

"We are telling the truth," Yeru said. "If you lead us back up to the entry chamber we can show you. There are others up there who are dangerous." Yeru thought about the Whute and her cult. "But if you help us defeat them and escape we can prove that the outside is safe."

Again those on the steps whispered amongst one another as Ikam sucked on her teeth, weighing them up. Yeru searched her face and saw something in those eyes. Was that hunger?

"Prove it," Ikam said.

"Take us to the entry chamber and we'll show you," Etan said.

The whispers rose to a mumble from those on the stairs. Yeru thought she caught the ancient word for *'demons'* amongst the babble. If they were supposed to be some kind of council for Ikam, Yeru wondered at their usefulness.

"This is impossible. If you have no other way to prove you are from outside we will have to throw you out of our home," Ikam said.

"But the stairs," Yeru said gesturing to the blockade behind Ikam. Yeru could tell it was man-made blockage and not a structural collapse of the steps beyond. They could remove enough of the rubble to allow them to squeeze through.

Ikam glanced over her shoulder as if she had forgotten the way up to the next floor was behind her. She raised an eyebrow then and more chatter came from the others. Ikam tapped on the arm of her throne until they silenced.

She sat forward on her throne and peered down at Yeru. "You must know that many of the stairs have been collapsed to stop the creatures from migrating and moving freely. To find a clear path from here to the entry chamber would take years of travelling the dangerous floors, if it is even possible."

Yeru's blood ran cold.

They had managed four floors until they had come across a blockage. To travel up one hundred and twenty three even four at a time before having to venture out onto the floors would take too long. They would starve long before they made it anywhere close to the entry chamber. Yeru had thought it was a one off occurrence but if these people had systematically destroyed the stairwells to stop the creatures from travelling between the floors…

They were doomed.

"There must be a way," Etan said.

Ikam's face softened and pity rounded her eyes as she shook her head. "It is not possible."

The elderly man who had cut Etan turned to Ikam and spoke. "*Sune brak a vatu?*"

That sounded awfully similar to the word for '*rise*' in the old tongue. Ikam's face darkened. "*Fenta so.*"

"What about the atrium? Can we climb up between the floors?" Etan pleaded, a nasally whine leaking into his voice.

The leader didn't dignify that with a response. "I'm afraid because we cannot confirm the floor you are from we will have to remove you from the city. We do not allow strangers within our walls."

A sinking feeling filled Yeru's gut as two guards swept in from behind them. They had no way of making it back up to the entry chamber. No way to escape. Panic swelled and bile rose up Yeru's throat as the room began to spin.

They were stuck. Trapped.

And Yeru would die down here.

The guards dragged them from the chamber as it erupted into chatter from the council on the steps. All the while Ikam watched with cold eyes.

9

A Scholar's Calling

"I think as scholars we're looking to the past to make sense of the world around us. We read about those who have lived to find meaning in our own lives."
                    - Yeru's Journal, page 26.

Yeru thought of her mother. She would never know what had happened to Yeru. Much like her father, Yeru would disappear from her life. Lost deep beneath the sand entombed within the very place she sought the most.

And Yeru would never find out if her father was alive. Was he out there similarly trapped? Yeru day-dreamed about setting off to find him and bringing her father home. But she was no adventurer and this just proved it. They were trapped in a library thought to be legend and they would die there.

She glanced at Etan as they were led back through the streets. His face was tight and drawn as he stared sightlessly at the ground. *You should have let him fall,* a voice whispered. If Yeru had let this fool fall, she wouldn't have been dragged down into the depths. And yet she found herself pushing back against the voice. If time were to return to that moment she would have done the same again. For if she had let Etan fall with a chance of saving him, Yeru would never be able to face her family again. It would have been a betrayal of herself. It was against her nature. The anger fizzled out in a sigh, leaving only coldness.

As they approached the walls of the settlement, a familiar voice called and the guards stopped. The elderly man who had stabbed Etan waved them down. He spoke with the guards as Yeru and Etan stood in wait.

Defeat held the silence between them. There was nothing to say. Guards moved atop the shelves around the walls ever surveying the library beyond. They had watch of the gates into the city but Yeru hadn't seen anyone approach the settlement to warrant the efforts. What were they so concerned about?

After a moment the guards shrugged and walked off, dismissed by the elder. The old man took a moment to weigh up Yeru and Etan before stepping forward. "Is it true?" he asked.

"Is what true?" Etan asked.

"Are you from outside?" the man asked.

Yeru was tired of the questioning. They had no way to prove it and so wordlessly nodded. The man stared into her eyes. Seemingly coming to a conclusion, he flicked his head back towards the settlement.

"Follow me."

He led them back into the strange city within the library. But instead of travelling down the main thoroughfare, the elder wandered into one of the side passages.

The buildings were pressed close together with what had once no doubt been aisles between the bookshelves and were now alleys and streets. Yeru marvelled at the homes built through and between the bookshelves. The people had found a way to utilise every bit of space available to them.

"My name is Otune," he said.

With a name that lengthy, the elderly man would be in a high social standing in Tarris. Yeru wondered if these people had the same naming conventions as the rest of the country. She knew other countries didn't correlate social standing to the length of one's name, but she had assumed being Tarrisian that these people would follow the same practices. And yet assumption can shroud truth in expectation.

"I am Yeru, and this is Etan."

Otune grunted and kept walking. Light orbs were more sporadic here with corners sitting in shadow. Fewer people walked these back streets but many still wore expressions ranging from curiosity to hostility as they passed. Finally they came to their destination at the dead end of one of the alleyways. A tarp covered the opening into one of the narrow homes. The walls were made of some treated leather and flexed when Yeru pressed it. Otune raised an eyebrow but didn't comment on her curiosity as he brushed the tarp aside and waved for them to enter. Yeru and Etan shared a glance. This could be a trap but if the man wanted them dead, he could have killed them with the dagger back in the cell they were held in. And what did they have to lose?

Inside was a narrow chamber with a long sofa and a staircase at the back of the room.

"Til!" Otune called following in after them. Stomping rung through the walls as someone ran and jumped down the floors until he appeared from the steps.

He looked to be in his early twenties with the unmistakable similarities in facial features that placed him as a relation to Otune. The same small nose and sharp jawline. A grandson, perhaps? *"Esan toru?"* he asked. His short brown hair bounced as he dropped to the ground.

"You must speak to the old tongue so that our guests can understand. But yes. This is them," Otune said. The elder turned to Yeru and Etan. "Tea? We have much to discuss."

The house was built with small narrow floors each having a purpose. There were sitting rooms, a kitchen and bedrooms each on their own level. Most of their utensils and belongings were made from leather. Which made sense as it was the one material those living in a library would have in troves.

They all huddled around a low table in one of the sitting rooms. There were no chairs, as a space saving measure Yeru guessed, and instead sat with their feet under the table upon a cushion as they sipped their tea. Yeru didn't know what was in the tea but it was earthy and flavourful after drinking nothing but water for what was likely days.

Til questioned Yeru and Etan about life outside the library as Otune prepared the tea. He was fascinated about the sky and openness of it all. Equally Yeru and Etan got to ask about life in the library. It wasn't as foreign as Yeru thought it would be. They had scouts go out and find them food and supplies as the city grew and flourished. Life was much like the early settlements in Tarris. The main differences being the creatures wandering the library. There were many different kinds. Most of which Yeru and Etan couldn't place by their descriptions that Til shared and so were likely new species. *Or old ones*, Yeru mused.

"Now that you believe us, can you talk to your leader about helping us get home?" Etan asked.

Til glanced down at the table and Otune cleared his throat. "I'm afraid once Ikam has made a decision, it's final. She will not help you."

Slumping forward, Etan shook his head. "We're going to die down here."

It was the first time either of them had said it aloud and hearing it voiced somehow made it more real.

"Now, now. We didn't say that." A smile crept onto Otune's face. "You happen to be talking to the settlement's expert in top floor research. Now granted, my main focus doesn't go above ten or so floors above us currently. But I have done some private study into higher floors, albeit from texts in the library."

It didn't surprise Yeru that the man was a scholar. Yeru supposed he was akin to the environmental scholars in Tansen. Otune looked like he was moving towards a point so neither Yeru nor Etan spoke as he stood and wandered over to a cupboard. He returned with a book and slammed it down onto the table.

"The entry chamber and outside is a passion project of mine," Otune said. "I have petitioned for us to travel higher up the floors for years but it's been deemed too dangerous."

"I thought it was impossible because of the stairwell blockages," Yeru said.

"Yes, by stairs it would be impossible. However," that smile crept back onto Otune's face, "there is a room that rises up the floors."

Otune opened the book and flicked through until he found the page he was looking for. Then he flipped the book around and pushed it towards Yeru and Etan. The book was ancient, the pages dotted with age and perished around the edges. But the illustrations and text were still bold and clear. It showed a room no larger than the small chamber they sat in now and beside it was a complex pulley system with multiple weights of different sizes allowing the room to rise and fall to align with different levels depending on which weight was released. Yeru had never seen anything like it. She faced Etan who sat wide eyed.

"And this exists in the library?" he asked.

"Not only that but we have a good idea of where it is," Til said grinning.

Otune's face tightened. "However its location is a bit of an issue. I have asked to create an expedition to find this rising room but Ikam has brought me to heel every time as it is likely in the dark wing of the library."

Etan barked out a laugh. "A dark wing? That's fine. We walked through many darkened parts of the library before your scouts found us."

Otune was shaking his head before Etan finished. "No. You came from the northern side. While some areas have no light, the dark wing is something else entirely. I only know of one person who survived travelling into the dark wing and he talked about the dark *moving*. He spoke of nightwalkers that were said to wear the faces of people. And of unspeakable horrors that he wouldn't put into words. The man was driven mad by the time we found him wandering near the entrance."

A shiver ran down Yeru's spine. "You thought we might be nightwalkers."

Otune and Til shared a glance and nodded. "They are said to be able to look human. Many ancient tomes reference beings of their nature and the only way to reveal them is that when cut they bleed smoke rather than blood."

"The dark wing is the one part of this floor that remains unexplored for that very reason. Generations past, they sent explorers there but only one company has set out that way in living memory. Of the thirty-three that entered, only one survived," Til said.

Etan clasped his hands and sat forward. "And that's where you think this rising room is?"

Otune nodded.

"Would it take us to the entry chamber?" Yeru asked.

Otune nodded again.

Yeru and Etan didn't need to speak. One shared look and they knew this was their only choice. It was die down here in the dark or push through the shadows to the light.

"Will you show us the way?" Yeru asked.

"I shall do more than that. I'm coming with you," Til said.

Yeru was about to raise an objection when Otune lifted a hand. "We will both come with you."

"I thought you said only one person has survived entering this wing?" Etan asked.

Otune sipped his tea. "We are scholars, are we not? It is our duty to wade into the dark. It is our duty to bring light to what no one has seen. Why did you venture into the library if outside is as peaceful as you say?"

Yeru opened her mouth and shut it again.

"Because there is living and there is *living*. A scholar hunts for truth. That is our calling. It's what brings life to our bones. And to think that there is another world out there." Otune looked up as if trying to peer through the miles upon miles of stone. "I must see it with my own eyes."

Yeru hadn't thought of scholars like that. She had always separated what she did and the adventuring her father did. But the way Otune put it made it sound like they were one and the same. Both ventured out into the unknown. Perhaps she was already the adventurer she wanted to be. Her mother's words echoed in her mind.

'That passion in your heart and that fire in your eyes. That's his. I can see it now burning away in there. That. That is what your father is like, that is what you're like.'

If Yeru peered hard enough, she too could see that passion in Otune's eyes. She turned to Etan who smiled back. "*There is living and there is living,* huh? Well, I'm not sure we'd survive long down here anyway," he said.

Yeru faced the elder and his grandson.

"When do we leave?"

10

The Wasteland of Bone and Grass

"My father told me that what is in history is often also true today. I fear he may be right."
                    - Yeru's Journal, page 211.

They spent another day within the settlement that Yeru learned was called *Erthu,* or Blackwood in the old tongue. Otune and Til went about collecting supplies and settling their affairs but they had no other family and few friends to say goodbye to. In that time, Yeru and Etan explored some of Blackwood and made comprehensive notes and sketches of the settlement with promises to return. However, the locals were still suspicious of them, so they didn't linger in any one place for too long.

They set off the next day resupplied and ready to face the library once more. No one stopped them. No one questioned them. Otune simply waved and the gates rose and they walked out into the dark.

The immediate area outside of Blackwood was swathed in darkness. Otune explained this was because some creatures were attracted to light. However after they passed through several bookshelf filled chambers, Otune passed out light orbs as well as a black cloth that was thick enough to smother the light completely, should they need to hide themselves.

"What are these light orbs?" Yeru asked as she walked alongside Otune.

He shrugged. "We don't know. They hold light almost indefinitely, from what we've found. It is rare to find one intact with no light."

Otune spoke casually as they moved through the bookshelves, unafraid of using his normal voice. Whereas Yeru couldn't bring herself to talk above a whisper as she searched the dark.

"However, where that energy is coming from, we do not know. The only true way to extinguish the light is to smash the orb but we are wary to do such a thing. They are a limited resource until we can learn how they function, and well…"

He didn't need to finish the thought. Life down here with no light would be a different nightmare. There was so much that they didn't understand.

Sporadically, Til bent over and inspected a paw print or a chewed bit of plant, tracking the wildlife around them Otune had explained. It was easier to avoid their nests if they could find where the animals were eating and trawling to and from. However it wasn't long until they came across the first horror from the shadows.

The many limbed beast scuttled across the high ceiling. Til brought a finger to his lips to silence them but made no indication to cover their light orbs so Yeru assumed the beast was blind and relied on sound to sense the world around it. The strange silence of the library made the creature impossible to hear until it was right above them. It moved with the sound of cracking bones. That was when Yeru noticed that its legs were the alabaster of skeleton. The monster had no skin.

Yeru's heart thundered in her chest as the creature stopped right above them. She held her breath and ducked despite it being high above. The others equally had frozen staring upward at it. Its head twitched unnaturally quickly with a *snap*. After a moment, it continued on its way crawling out of sight. It wasn't until Til moved first that Yeru sucked in a breath.

"What was that?" Etan asked.

"Skelcrawler," Til said. "They can't see but they have sensitive hearing. If it were any closer I'd have had us move away in case it heard our heartbeats."

Nausea bubbled in Yeru's gut. Heard her heartbeat? She was glad she had held her breath as it grew near. It was no doubt an evolutionary trait. When a creature cannot see and relies on its hearing in a place that suppresses sound, it would need to have incredibly powerful hearing to pick up its prey.

The blood drained from Etan's face. Til grimaced. "It won't be the last skelcrawler we see and there's worse in the dark wing, that's for sure."

Time was difficult to judge in the library but Yeru estimated they had been wandering its chambers for the better part of three hours. Some sections were well lit with many light orbs revealing the bookshelves and reading nooks. However, most of the floor was dark with no light beyond that which they brought.

The quiet was smothering. Yeru listened as they moved but it was as if they were alone deep within the lost library. A fact disproven by Til who often signalled them to hide as another creature stalked past.

At the end of a long straight lined with shelves was a colossal ceiling to floor door. The door looked to be made for giants. Yeru wondered at how the ancients opened and closed such a huge door and was grateful that it was left slightly ajar when Til pointed to it as their destination.

"Past here is the dark wing," Otune said as they

reached the end of the chamber. "This is your last chance to turn around. Once we have entered, it is unlikely you will have another."

Yeru and Etan shared a glance before nodding to Otune. They did not hesitate as doing so would have shackled them to anticipation and worry. Yeru had to get home. And so together, they slid through the opening and into the black.

The chamber beyond was shrouded in darkness. Yeru lifted her orb but she couldn't make out the ceiling above.

"There are no bookshelves," Etan whispered.

He was right. The area around them was stark and empty aside from pillars rising into the dark above.

"There are further in," Til said. "But watch your feet here."

The tiled floor was made of smooth marble but knee high grass and plant life had grown through the cracks and seams around the tiles. Through the reeds, Yeru could make out ornate designs and carvings around the edges of the cracked planes. But most were fragmented making it impossible to see the full piece.

They pushed further into the dark wing and Yeru understood where the name had come from. The chamber was unlike any they had been in so far. So wide and tall that their light orbs couldn't touch the faces of the room. It left Yeru feeling open and vulnerable within a wide expanse of shadow.

They trod slowly and quietly, eyes searching the dark. There was a clatter and Etan yelped. Spinning, Yeru reached for her dagger but Til was already at his side. Etan was staring at something by his foot. Then he lifted his light orb and his face somehow grew even paler.

"What is it?" Yeru hissed.

"Bodies," Otune said.

Stepping up beside Etan, Yeru peered out and saw that Otune was right. Amongst the still grass were skeletons clad in armour. There had to have been hundreds. Perhaps thousands. Yeru and Etan had come across some skeletons in the library but nothing like this. It was a wasteland of bone and grass, remnants of a battlefield fought upon.

"We believe there was a battle in the library at the time of the Darkening," Otune said.

Yeru swallowed, her mouth having suddenly gone dry. This had to have been the site of a large scale battle. But who had been fighting?

"The Darkening?" Etan asked.

"The day mankind fled into the depths of the library," Otune said. His face was grim. "Or we thought all of mankind had."

For once Yeru was glad for the strange noise suppression in the library. Otherwise their words would be echoing in the hall around them.

"Do you know who was fighting?" Yeru asked as they continued through the dark wing, careful to step around the bones of the dead.

Otune stared forward as he shook his head. "We have records of other chambers on other floors having similar battlefields, but none speak of who had been fighting. All the bodies are human and wearing the same types of armour. So perhaps one another? A civil war some guess."

"Or something that couldn't die," Etan said.

After another hour of walking, Yeru was beginning to wonder if the dark wing wasn't as dangerous as Otune and Til had thought when movement stirred. Til gestured to mask their orbs. So Yeru wrapped hers in the darkened cloth and pressed herself against the closest pillar.

Darkness.

Silence.

Faintly, footsteps approaching.

Yeru held her breath and forced her eyes shut. She couldn't see anything anyway.

"Yeru."

Yeru opened her eyes to the black. She slid the cover off the orb just enough to allow some of the light to escape.

Etan stood in front of her.

Yeru smothered a yelp as she stepped back, tripping on a skull and was sent sprawling. Bone remains cracked on impact. She looked up at Etan who was standing strangely, watching her. He didn't have his light orb in his hands. She was about to admonish him for creeping up on her when she heard someone speak.

"Yeru? What're you doing?" It was Etan's voice but it had come from *behind her*.

Yeru's blood ran cold. The Etan in front of her grinned and his face began to melt into darkness.

She screamed then, kicking backward. Hands dragged Yeru to her feet and they were running. It was a blur of darkness and pillars. White hot panic kept her moving. Feet crunched through bones as they fled.

The dark around them seemed to coalesce, contracting and pulsing. And within it shapes moved. Indistinct faces formed and faded. Terror had Yeru by the throat making it hard to breathe.

With caution thrown to the wind, they pushed back the darkness with the light of their orbs. Etan was at her side. But they had lost Otune and Til at some point.

Bolting through the chamber they weaved through the pillars. Yeru's stomach dropped as her foot caught on some remains but she managed to keep to her feet. Finally, they reached a wall and Yeru saw a door.

"There!" she called.

They burst through into the next room and slammed it shut behind them.

Nothing stirred.

Yeru crept back, orb pointed at Etan.

"Is it really you?" she asked.

Etan furrowed his brow, perplexed by the question. He was holding his orb but the nightwalker could have stolen one from the others in the chaos.

"What do you mean?" he asked.

"Cut your hand." It was the only way that Yeru knew to prove that it was truly him. She wasn't sure if nightwalkers could capture memories or thoughts so questions may have been useless.

"Cut your hand!" Yeru screamed the words now. She couldn't shake that dark Etan with the melting face.

Eyes wide, Etan raised his hands. "Okay." He slid his dagger from his belt and cut his palm. Blood welled.

Yeru had to fight back tears. "It had your face, Etan. I'm sorry. I'm so sorry."

"Hey, hey. It's okay." He swept her into an embrace. "It's me."

They stood there for a moment as Yeru composed herself. "Did you not see them?" Yeru asked as she withdrew.

"I saw shapes but that's it."

"They can look like us. I thought—" Yeru's heart started to batter in her chest again. She took a deep breath. "I thought it was you but its face dispersed into shadow."

"Nightwalkers." Etan's face hardened and Yeru nodded. "Did you see Otune or Til?"

"Not after we hid our orbs," Yeru said.

"Damn it," Etan said. "How are we going to find our way to this rising room without them?"

Yeru clutched the light orb closer. After several breathes she turned towards Etan. "We need to go back in." She couldn't leave the others and Yeru had seen Otune's map, they could spend days wandering the dark wing without finding the right room. Yeru knew they wouldn't last that long even with the map.

"Are you mad?" Etan stared at her. "We barely made it out."

"It could get worse from here. And I don't like the idea of wandering this dark wing without an idea of where we're going."

It was quiet. Yeru was beginning to hate that quiet. Once silence had been her sanctuary. But now it had become her prison. In the Tansen Archives it was a settling of the world around her but in here it was the absence of the world. A void. There was an emptiness to the quiet that unsettled Yeru.

Etan took a moment to mull their choices over but he knew they would die without Otune guiding them and so he steeled himself and gave a nod. "Okay. But we stick beside each other."

"The light seemed to repel them," Yeru said. "It didn't want to get too near when I uncovered the orb. We can use that."

Rolling his shoulders, Etan moved back to the door. "We keep moving. Stay close to the pillars and run if we see one of those things."

Etan counted down on his fingers and threw the door open. Brandishing her light orb, Yeru waved it to ward off the dark.

Nothing stood on the other side of the door. Only stillness and the black.

They crept in slowly, orbs held high. Following the cracked skeletons of their heedless sprint through the chamber, they retraced their steps.

"Otune," Yeru called out. "Til."

As they moved further through the chamber there was a light. One of the orbs lay discarded in the grass. Yeru and Etan shared a concerned glance and moved towards it. As they approached they saw something moving in the grass beside it.

"Otune!" Yeru called.

They ran to his side. The old man lay on his back staring sightlessly at the dark above. He was mumbling to himself. Wary, Yeru surveyed the area around them but everything was still. A cut lined Otune's cheek and blood dripped down his face. It was him.

"Otune?" Yeru asked. His eyes shot over to meet

hers.

"Is it really you?" His voice was strained and weak.

"Yes, yes. It's us. Come on." She turned to Etan. "Help me get him up."

Together they pulled the older man to a seated position against the pillar. He seemed to come back to himself but still his eyes shot back and forth at the black around them.

"Where is Til?" Etan asked.

"I… I…" Otune put a hand to his head. "I don't know. I thought it was one of them. There were so many. They smiled and chased us and…"

Etan glanced over to Yeru. "We need to get out of here. We can't linger."

"I know, I know," Yeru said.

The elderly man was clearly rattled but they were wasting time. "Where did you last see Til?"

Yeru had to repeat herself before Otune looked at her and understanding lit his eyes. He pointed a bony finger past her shoulder. Following his gesture, Yeru saw something at the limits of their light.

"Keep an eye on him," Yeru said and wandered towards it.

"Yeru! We said we were sticking together," Etan hissed.

"I'll be one moment."

She trod carefully through the field of bones, her light orb banishing the curling shadows at her feet. Soon she saw boots.

Was that Til?

The dark was thicker here. It shouldn't have been possible, but the light didn't penetrate as deeply into the smog-like cloud filling the chamber.

Yeru stepped up and held out her orb. Til lay dead on the ground, eyes glazed and blood trickling out of his mouth. Yeru clasped a hand over her mouth to stop herself from screaming. Whatever had killed him had stabbed him though the gut, his tunic soaked through with blood. She wanted to turn and run back to the others but something made her stay, a familiar shape. A strange bent blade lay beside the body. Yeru picked it up. It was Til's blade.

No, it couldn't be. Til had his attached to his belt. So, this must have been Otune's blade.

The sickening realisation brought bile up Yeru's throat.

Otune's words rang in her head. *I thought it was one of them. There were so many.*

Had he killed his grandson after mistaking him for one of the nightwalkers?

Yeru stumbled holding back tears. That couldn't be true. She hadn't known Til long but she felt partly responsible for this. They were only here because of Etan and her. A tremor ran down her arm as Yeru inhaled and inhaled trying to catch a breath that escaped her.

"Yeru!" Etan's voice was urgent. She spun to see him drawing back into the chamber with Otune at his side as another figure stood by Otune's discarded light orb.

The head snapped in her direction.

It wore *her face*. A rictus grin betraying her as not human.

The nightwalker kicked the light orb into a pillar shattering it to pieces, plunging them into darkness.

11

The Scholar's Schism

"The scholar must wander past the shelves of their library to know the world within its pages."
                - Yeru's Journal, page 197.

Yeru brought her light orb up as the shadows shot towards her. She screamed waving Otune's blade and the orb as she ran. Faces flexed against the fabric-like black. She saw her own. Her mother's. Her father's. Scholar Sciona's. Isin's. They all grinned at her from the tunnel of shadows closing in around her as faces swirled in a vortex of dark echoes.

Yeru almost crashed into Etan and Otune who were ambling through the chamber, weaving amongst the pillars. Bones crunched beneath their feet and the shadows screamed, pressing in. Yeru swished the light orb at any tendrils of darkness and they shrunk back into the mass around them. Whispers hid within the screams coming from the dark. They were incomprehensible under the shrieking that rattled in Yeru's skull not letting a thought form through the horror that held her.

"The door!" Etan shouted.

Part of Yeru knew that a door couldn't hold back this demon in the dark. But the drive to get something solid between prey and predator rang in her mind.

They burst through the door and shoved it closed behind them. Otune fell to the ground as Yeru and Etan threw their weight against the door. Yeru waited to be thrown back, for the door to explode and the dark to seep in and drown them.

And yet it never came.

There was stillness.

Their ragged breaths were all that could be heard. After a moment, Yeru realised there was no force pressing against the door either. She released her grip and Etan watched in terror but the door didn't shift. So he, too, let go and the door remained closed. Yeru searched the dark. Was it already in here with them?

"Where did it go?" Etan asked.

"It's toying with us," Otune whispered. He sat up, drawing his legs up to his chest and rocking like a child might.

"What do you mean?" Yeru asked.

"We need to keep moving. It could appear at any moment," Etan hissed.

The old man stared, eyes wide. "It made me. It appeared and… And it… I thought it was my grandson. It was playing with us like toys. Pitting us against one another. It *knew*. How did it know?"

He began to rock faster.

"It's okay, Otune," Yeru said. She dropped to her haunches beside him and rubbed his back.

Otune went rigid. "I killed him. I killed my grandson."

"*What?*" Etan asked.

Yeru tightened her grip around Otune's shoulder

as she gave Etan a look that said '*not now*'. "It tricked you. *It* killed Til, Otune. Not you. But we need to keep moving." The old man didn't look to be in any state to walk, but they couldn't linger. Not with the nightwalkers around.

He shook his head. "Go on without me."

"No, we can't leave you," Yeru said.

A tear rolled down his cheek as he glanced away. "It's straight from here if the maps are to be believed. Through a shelved wing containing journals."

"We aren't leaving you, Otune," Yeru said. But the old man wouldn't meet her eyes. She glanced at Etan for support and he, too, looked away. "No. I refuse. What happened to learning the truth? Venturing out?"

Neither of them said anything.

Yeru's grip tightened around Otune's curved blade as frustration bubbled up. She had forgotten that she was holding it. There was something strangely familiar about the shape. Recognition clicked in her mind and Yeru gasped. The other two stared at her as Yeru pulled out her journal attached to her waist. Finding the right page, she ran a finger down her notes until she came to a symbol that was the same shape as the weapon. The blade was the same as the marking on Ma-nivi's murals. The very symbol that she had been studying all those months ago in the Tansen Archives trying to learn its meaning.

"Otune what is this weapon?" Yeru asked holding up the curved blade.

The sight of it pained Otune and he cringed away from it. "The scholar's schism. We use it when exploring the library. If you throw it, the blade can slice through a target and return to you like a boomerang."

"Why would Ma-nivi's illustrations of learning include a *weapon*?" Yeru mused.

A warning? Perhaps it was written beside pieces of knowledge that could lead to danger?

"No," Yeru said. That didn't add up. There were too

many uses of it. Etan asked her a question but Yeru was too focused to hear his words. Then it slid into place.

"The passing of knowledge," Yeru said.

"What?" Etan asked.

Yeru held out her notes and pointed to the symbol. "This marking is found all over Ma-nivi's murals when it shows the deity passing on knowledge to the people. I have been trying to figure out what it means for years."

"It's the same shape," Etan said pointing to the scholar's schism.

"Exactly! I think it's used when the knowledge has to be passed on by *doing*. By seeing. By being in the danger. I think it means that you need to partake and see it to truly understand it," Yeru said. "Like you were saying back in Blackwood, Otune."

'*There are some things that words cannot contain. Sights that must be seen to be understood. Sounds that must be heard to truly know them,*' he had said.

It took falling into a library lost to the ages and finding a splinter civilization of Tarrisians locked beneath miles of stone to make sense of a simple marking. There was little chance Yeru would have figured out the meaning from the books in the archive. But that was the point, was it not? One had to take the leap into the unknown.

The scholar must wander past the shelves of their library to know the world within its pages.

Yeru's resolve hardened. "I am sorry about Til." Again, she clasped the elderly man's shoulder reassuringly. "It was not your fault. And you will see him again in the Reed Fields of Aru, in the next life. And when you do, what will you tell him? I gave up and sat in the library until death found me? Or will you venture out and learn the truth? Will you find him in the next life and tell him of all the knowledge you found and brought to light as a scholar? Will you help all those in Blackwood?

"Show him that his sacrifice wasn't in vain," Yeru said.

It was impossible to tell the thoughts behind Otune's tired eyes.

There was a breath of silence and he nodded.

"You're right. Til would want me to go on. For us to go on." Otune sucked in a breath, tears still damp on his cheeks as he clambered to his feet and Yeru offered him back his schism. "No. Keep it."

She was about to say that she barely knew how to use her dagger, but his pained expression as he looked at the weapon that he killed his grandson with stayed her hand. Attaching it to her belt, Yeru turned deeper into the library.

"This way," Otune said.

The following chamber was much like the others with ceiling to floor bookshelves lined in rows and wide walkways between. There was no light aside from that which they cast. However, the dark here acted as it should. It wasn't thicker than it should be and it didn't pulse or shift.

Skeletons still littered the floor among the grass but there were fewer than in the pillared chamber. Perhaps that other room was where some final standoff had occurred. There was no way of knowing. And yet as Yeru felt the cold steel of the blade bounce on her thigh, she thought that there might one day.

They trailed by the edges, staying close to the shelves and avoiding the open areas. Moving in silence, they searched the shadows. The plush rug indicating the main thoroughfare veered right and they turned the corner into an atrium, revealing the darkened floors above and beneath. And on the far side, around the circular balustrade blocking the fall, was a double door that matched the sketch in Otune's book.

"That's it," Otune said, wonder in his voice. He stepped forward but Etan laid a hand on his chest.

"You said that thing was toying with us. We need to be careful," Etan said.

Avoiding the railing of the atrium, they walked around the edges of the bookshelves.

"Once we get in, will you know how to work the moving room?" Etan asked Otune.

"Yes, it's a complicated pulley system but I have studied it for years and know it like the back of my hand." He stared at the double doors. "I never thought I'd get to see it, though."

Yeru couldn't help but smile at the joy it brought the old man. Then she watched as his face darkened and mouth fell agape.

"Til?" he asked the dark.

Past him was a shadow.

It was here.

"Otune!" Yeru called. She reached forward to grab him but a rush of black wind separated them as Otune disappeared down the aisle towards the shape.

Backing up from the smog of shadow, Yeru realised that it was behind her too. Breath catching in her throat, she lifted the light orb and some of the dark cowered back.

Etan shouted but his words were smothered by the hissing of the black wind that rushed in. Yeru realised that there was a limit to the shadows dislike of the light. She couldn't force it back enough to let her rejoin her friends.

Faces started to form within the dark once more. It was closing in.

She had to get away.

One part of the shadow was thinner than the rest and she charged pushing through it and broke into a sprint.

Bookshelves surrounded her as she ran through the aisles. Yeru burst into an open reading space with chairs and loose pages scattered across the wide expanse. No darkness chased her and she could no longer hear Otune or Etan. She couldn't have run far. It was likely the noise suppression of the library shutting her off from the others.

Yeru set off in the last direction she had seen Otune. She had to stop him from going near that nightwalker.

Skulking back between the shelves, Yeru heard the clatter of bones. Instinct took over and she barrel rolled to the side as a skelcrawler crashed into the ground where she had been standing. Its legs snapped and popped out of place as the too-human face shot up to look at her. Yeru screamed and threw the scholar's schism. It spun through the air and smacked the creature, knocking it back into the bookshelf. Then the schism circled back. Yeru jumped to grab it but missed catching the weapon and it embedded itself into the shelf behind her. She pulled at the schism but it was buried deep in the wood.

The skelcrawler cracked and snapped as the bones slid back into place. It pushed its body up and the head creaked as it moved back into position atop its too-many limbs.

"Come on!" Yeru shouted as she continued to pry the schism from the shelf.

The creature hissed and leapt as Yeru yanked the blade free. It swung in a wide arc as she fell back and the skelcrawler slid over the top of it, a slice running along the bone of one of its limbs. It crashed into the shelf and broke apart with the rattle of bones smashing against stone. Yeru didn't wait to see if it was going to put itself back together again and bolted down the aisle.

The sound of blood pumping filled her ears as her heart's frantic beating threatened to give out.

Skidding to a stop, she saw Otune standing in the atrium alone. In front of him was the shadow of Til.

"Otune!" As she approached, she heard the old man crying.

"Yeru! Help!" Etan's voice rang above the crying.

Turning, she saw Etan pressed against the railing with the darkness edging towards him. He was going to topple over the balustrade. Yeru looked between the two before sprinting for Etan.

"Otune, it's not real!" she shouted as she threw the scholar's schism at the shadow of Til, unsure if the creature had a tangible body.

Yeru dove in between Etan and the wall of shadow brandishing her light orb like a torch. It lurched back and Yeru stepped up beside Etan.

"We need to help Otune!" Yeru said still waving the orb.

"Yeru?"

She looked up to see Etan run out of one of the aisles, confusion lining his face. Yeru's froze, ice in her veins. She peered out the corner of her eye and the Etan standing beside her grinned.

Terror held her in place as pain ran up her side. She glanced down to see blood, *her blood*, staining her robes.

"Yeru!" Etan screamed.

The world spun around her as she stumbled. Darkness burst through her side and blood spattered the railing. She dropped her light orb and fell back. The nightwalker held that too-long grin as it advanced toward her. There was nothing behind those dead eyes. How had she thought that this was Etan? There was no life there. No brightness that shone from the living. Those corpse eyes bore down on her. Its body dispersed into shadow but that face remained pooled in shadow. Pointed tendrils formed and the smile widened.

Swish.

The scholar's schism flew past Yeru. Then it burst through the shadow. The nightwalker broke apart for a moment but then reformed. No blade could stop this creature. Etan failed.

Yeru thought of the cult that had been sabotaging

scholars researching the past. Was this why? Did they know the horrors that the library held?

The schism returned, zipping through the creature's lower half. Both the nightwalker and Yeru watched the weapon as it continued its trajectory heading for the light orb.

SMASH.

Light exploded. An ear shattering squeal came from the nightwalker and then hands were under Yeru dragging her away. She watched as the nightwalker writhed in pain. Her vision swam. Whether from the explosion or blood loss Yeru couldn't tell. Clutching at her side, Yeru put her unsteady feet beneath her as Etan drew her up.

The flash faded and only Etan's light orb was left to light the dim atrium.

The darkness pulled itself together reforming. To their left, the clatter of a skelcrawler sounded from the bookshelves.

"We need to go! Now!" Etan shouted and then they were moving.

"Otune," Yeru managed between sharp breaths.

The old man was clambering onto the railing. The shadow of Til hovered over the drop, a smile fixed onto that stretched face. It was trying to make him jump.

"Otune!" Etan shouted. He didn't seem to hear as he stood on the balustrade.

They ran to help him.

The room bulged and stretched in Yeru's vision but she didn't let up. A tear rolled down Otune's face. Yeru couldn't hear the words but read *'I'm sorry'* on the man's lips.

Til did not answer.

Otune reached for his dead grandson. His fingers trailed through the nightwalker and Otune fell into the dark abyss.

Yeru clasped her hand over her mouth to stifle a scream.

"Keep going!" Etan shouted yanking her hand to stop her from slowing. The shadow Til looked at her, the ever-present grin upon the creature's face before it dispersed into a cloud of darkness.

Then the torrent of shadow lurched towards them.

Etan pulled Yeru down and a skelcrawler launched itself over the top of them and crashed into the railing. They were so close to the door leading to the moving room now.

Darkness coiled around Yeru's ankle. She yelped, her heart launching into her throat as it pulled her back. Etan spun and shoved the light orb at the thin tendril. It burst like a puff of smoke. Then Etan grabbed Yeru's hand once more and they ran.

Yeru and Etan threw themselves at the double door. If it was locked, they would be dead in seconds. Luckily it flew open and they forced it shut behind them. Unlike before, this time the dark smashed into the door. The hinges bent with a groan.

"Find the pulley!" Etan called taking up position in the middle of the double doors allowing Yeru to step away. The room was small and on the far side was an opening revealing a line of individual ropes.

Adrenaline brought clarity to her blurry sight. She pulled at them one by one but nothing happened.

"I don't know how it works!" Yeru shouted. It was supposed to be Otune that worked the mechanism. He was dead now, Yeru reminded herself. They would be too if she didn't get it to work.

He had said it was complex and that he had studied it for years. But Yeru had to figure it out in seconds or the shadows would burst open that door and kill them both.

Etan hissed as the dark battered against the thick metal door. "Yeru, you need to hurry!"

Something in his voice made her turn. Swirling shadows snuck beneath the door. They reached out, wrapping around Etan's legs. Terror frenzied through

Yeru with an icy touch. She stared at the ropes. It was a pulley system. Those worked with simple physics. It didn't matter how complex the mechanism was, the theory was the same. Heavy weight dropped and lifted them up.

Yeru took her dagger and started cutting the ropes. The first snapped with a vicious *thwack* and shot up out of sight. The room didn't move. She cut the next. Nothing.

"Yeru!" Etan shouted.

Cut.

Nothing.

"Yer—"

Cut.

Snap.

The room lurched and shot upward. The sudden jerk threw Yeru back against the wall and she saw the darkness had a hold of Etan. It wrapped around his mouth and face. The room whistled upward as Yeru grabbed the railing. The shadows thinned and drew back until Etan fell to the ground freed. Not enough of the nightwalker had made it into the room, Yeru guessed. It could spread itself out but it was still one being.

Momentum pinned Yeru to the ground as they shot upward at incredible speed. Eventually, the room shuddered to an abrupt stop. Both Yeru and Etan were thrown against the ceiling and then crashed back into the floor.

A sharp fiery pain shot up Yeru's side. Her eyes bulged as her side burned leaving a woozy feeling. Yeru thought she might throw up but the sensation passed. Then Etan was at her side, his face a grimace as he looked at her wound.

"You did it," he said forcing a smile.

"We're going to be okay."

12

A Torch to Light Others

"Time is an echo. A reflection. I have learnt as much about myself as I have of those who came before from the past."
\- Yeru's Journal, page 228.

The doors slid open to reveal the atrium one floor below the entry chamber. Etan helped Yeru out of the moving room and sat her down, inspecting her wounded side. Yeru hissed as she slid her tunic up.

Slowing her breathing, Yeru took in their surroundings. Unlike deep within the library most of the light orbs here were lit casting a pale glow over the shelves. Otune and Til would never see that light. They were born and they died in the dark. They would never see the Sun Eye's gaze or the open deserts of Tarris. They would never feel the wind upon their faces.

But it wasn't just Otune and Til, generations had known nothing but the deep black of the library. Yeru took some solace in the fact that they didn't know of the world beyond. They didn't know that they lived in a nightmare.

She wasn't sure when the tears started and brushed one from her cheek.

"I've patched it up as best I can," Etan said. "You'll have to be careful not to move too much until this is stitched up."

Etan caught her staring back at the lift and his face softened. "We'll go back for them. Otune and Til's sacrifice won't be in vain. We'll help the rest."

Yeru nodded.

They made their way to the staircase and up to the first floor. Creeping up the stairwell, they listened for sounds of fighting or talking but the noise suppression of the library left nothing to be heard. The staircase came out near where the scholars had set up camp.

Yeru moved books to the side and peered through the bookshelf. The camp sat empty and still.

"Where are they?" Yeru asked.

"The plan I heard was that they would knock everyone out and steal their findings so that they could claim the discovery," Etan said.

Yeru turned on him. "They lied to you. Come on."

The tents were undamaged and nothing was disturbed. They skulked amongst the camp and glanced into the tents but no one was there. As they approached the main entrance, voices could be heard.

People sat around fires and ate in the cavern outside of the library. It didn't take Yeru long to realise they weren't from Whute's cult. She spotted none that had been involved in the cult's plot. Provisions were handed out and the wounded were being cared for.

Isin carried a bowl of food. She froze as she spotted Yeru. Isin dropped the bowl and it shattered against the stone. Then others glanced over at Yeru and Etan as Isin tore across the space and swept Yeru into a hug.

"I thought you were dead." Her words came out as a whimper. Yeru winced as how tightly Isin held her.

She had never heard the woman sad, much less teary.

"I'm okay. Are you?" Yeru asked.

Isin sniffed and pulled back, her eyes red. "I am thanks to you. I'm only a little mad that you made me throw up for a day straight. But compared to the other option…" Her voice trailed off and that was when Yeru noticed how few scholars, guards and assistants were in the entry chamber.

"The rest?" Etan asked and Isin shook her head. There must have been half of those who had been at the site before Yeru and Etan had fallen.

"Whute?" Yeru asked.

"Gone," Isin said and her face dropped. "And they collapsed the entrance."

Yeru's stomach dropped as she looked to the back of the cavern where the sandfall had been. Now there were rocks and boulders blocking the way.

"We were lucky they didn't bring down the entire chamber," Isin said. "We tried to move the rocks but it's no use. They are too heavy and we're worried it might still bring down the cavern if we move too much. So, we've just been…" She waved at the sorry souls huddled in groups. They had given up. The life and passion behind their eyes had gone out.

"What happened to you?" Isin asked.

"It's a long story," Etan said.

"Well, there's plenty time to tell it." She gestured to the chamber.

They had crawled through the Duat-damned depths of a lost library to be trapped in a cave?

Otune and Til and all of these scholars and guards and assistants dead with no retribution?

No, Yeru thought. She wouldn't allow that.

"Yeru?" Isin asked.

Yeru pushed past her and walked to the middle of the chamber. She clambered atop one of the benches and cleared her throat. Most of the people sat in defeated silence and so it took only moments for their attention to fall on her.

"So, is this it?" she shouted. Yeru looked around the room but no one would meet her gaze. "Are you just going to wait until death takes you? Starvation or dehydration?"

The scholars shifted uncomfortably.

"If we try to move the rocks the entire chamber will collapse," one of them said. "We should wait and hope someone comes to help us."

Yeru rounded on the man. "Do you not think that the ones who blocked us in thought of that? They won't let anyone come near here. They'll come up with a reason to dissuade them."

The scholars were used to controlled environments. They were used to their books and scrolls. So now that physical forces impeded their progress they looked to those who were better suited. Yeru supposed it made sense. She would have done the same thing not a couple of days ago but after seeing the horrors of what the world hid, after seeing what scholars must bring to light, Yeru realised that they didn't have the luxury of passing on the responsibility.

"We have a room of the smartest people in all of Tarris! If we work together, we can find a way out." Some of the scholars seemed emboldened by her words but others remained sceptical. They had to see that this was their duty.

Yeru hopped off the bench and wandered to the walls of the library of Nenelan. They watched her in silence as she approached the mural of Ma-nivi, deity of knowledge. She pointed to a small curved symbol, the shape of the scholar's schism. The very marking that had perplexed Yeru for months.

"Do you see this marking? I have been trying to decipher it for months. It wasn't until we fell into the depths of the library and found a community of people did I learn its meaning."

There were gasps at the revelation. Mumbled voices

said it was impossible, and that people couldn't have survived in the library.

"It's true," Etan said.

To share such a finding was what so many of the scholars in the room had been fighting against. To pass that undiscovered knowledge freely opened Yeru to losing the credit for the finding. But they had to see that it was about more than having a name in the histories.

"They have an ancient weapon called the scholar's schism. A curved throwing blade that matches this shape. Scholars used to explore and learn. To push to new boundaries. To learn the truth, we have to be more than what we have become. This is proof that scholars from ages past were much more than what we are today. We found knowledge through action. We did more than study scriptures and books. We *found* the secrets of the world ourselves."

Yeru had all of their attention now. One by one the flame behind their eyes flickered back to life. The fire her mother said she could see in Yeru and her father.

A passion that could light others' torches. Like her father had done for her.

"But how can we get out?" a voice called.

"That's simple," Yeru said. "We're going to make the library move again."

Groups of scholars had already looked at trying to learn the mechanisms of the library moving but none had figured it out. But as a team? As a team they would learn the secrets of the library. If they banded together instead of hiding their findings from one another, Yeru was confident that they could do anything.

A young scholar stood. "I am with you."

Then another stood and bowed. Then another. And another.

Soon, the surviving scholars, guards and assistants began work on moving the ancient library once more. The chamber filled with talk of all of their findings.

Teams blended and grouped together in areas of expertise. From passing notes, to drawing sketches, to teams searching the books on the shelves for answers, and those who ventured out into the floor to find the working mechanisms, all helped in whatever way they could.

And two days later, the library shook to life.

Yeru had been back in Tansen for no longer than a couple hours when Scholar Sciona sent for her. She was ushered through the halls of the palace and to the head scholar's office with haste.

Yeru stepped into the study. Morning light poured in the grand window as dust motes glinted under the Sun Eye's gaze.

"When I asked you to check if it was the library of Nenelan, I didn't expect you to bring it to me to prove it." Sciona's voice came from the rows of shelves in her study. Her collection had been so impressive the first time Yeru had seen it, but her study was a grain of sand in the desert compared to the depths of the library.

Sciona came out of the shelves clad in her scholar's robes and gestured to the table that they had sat in all those weeks ago. This time she did not offer tea but sat forward, hands clasped. "Tell me everything."

And so Yeru did.

Scholar Sciona kept her face impassive and unreadable as Yeru told her tale. It wasn't until she had finished that Sciona nodded and chewed on the inside of her lip in thought.

"To think, people have been living in the library for tens of thousands of years," Sciona said.

"If I may head scholar, I'd like to start a team to try and help those people," Yeru said but Sciona was shaking her head before she had finished.

"If what you said is true, it is too dangerous. We need to be careful about this."

"But—"

Sciona raised a hand. "I didn't say never, Yeru, but we have more pressing matters first. And we must approach entering further into the library with the upmost care as you have proven."

Yeru supposed that was the best she could have hoped for. She was going to need a lot of resources to help those people. It wasn't something that could be solved in mere weeks.

"Those creatures… nightwalkers can't be allowed out into Tarris," Sciona said.

Flashes of those smiling faces. Of Otune stepping off the railing to his death. She was right. The nightwalkers couldn't be let loose. She wouldn't let those monsters terrorize people.

"You're right." Yeru bowed in acquiescence. When she raised her head, she saw Sciona staring at her as if she were a puzzle to be solved.

"How did you do it?" Sciona asked.

"Do what?" Yeru asked.

Sciona tapped on the table. "None of the other scholar teams have come forward with findings or staked claims to the library's discoveries. In fact, several have pointed to you as the scholar with the findings."

Yeru blushed. She hadn't meant for it but she fell into a managerial role to help the scholars all work together and figure out how to move the library.

"They're citing you as the leading scholar of the library," Sciona said. "This is unprecedented. Usually there are papers upon papers of what scholars have found and staking claims to different research findings. But there's nothing. Silence. As if they're waiting for your report first."

Sciona raised an eyebrow but Yeru didn't know what to say.

She then cleared her throat and continued. "Because of this I want to put you in charge of the research teams looking into the library."

Yeru gawked.

She had expected Sciona herself to take the mantle of such an important position.

"I don't know what to say," Yeru stammered.

"Yes?" Sciona offered.

"Yes, of course." A shrill laugh escaped her. "I'd be honoured. Thank you, Scholar Sciona."

"Good," Sciona said. She sat back and looked Yeru up and down. "It changed you."

Yeru didn't need to ask what she meant, and simply nodded.

"I understand," Sciona said but Yeru wasn't sure she did. She wasn't sure anyone apart from Etan ever could. Facing that dark shadowy version of herself would remain in her nightmares until the end of her days.

"If I may, Scholar Sciona, is there any word on the cult?" Yeru asked.

The head scholar blew out a breath. "Sadly not. Whute and her cohort have crawled back to wherever they reared their heads from. Of course, the Rizu scholars are taking no accountability and claiming they had no contact with a woman of her description."

"Do you think…" Yeru's voice trailed off as she realised what she was about to ask.

"That the Rizu scholars and perhaps even the monarch are in contact with this cult?" Sciona held her hands out. "I don't know. It's a dangerous game to start pointing fingers without proof but fear not, we are actively looking for them. When they show their faces again, they will face justice."

Yeru had left out the fact that Etan had been one of those members that had been in on the plan to knock out and kill the other scholars. She had to believe that he hadn't known what they were capable of.

"But go, rest. I don't need your report today. I have already locked down the library with armed guards. It'll be safe until you're rested," Sciona said.

It was then that Yeru felt exhaustion seep into her

bones. Her body ached and the wound at her side flared hot despite having mostly healed.

"Thank you, Scholar Sciona." Yeru stood, bowed, and headed for the door.

"And Yeru," Sciona called. Yeru stopped and turned. "Congratulations." A smile crept across Sciona's face. Yeru nodded in thanks and left the study.

After passing through the scholar's wing of the palace, Yeru slowed and placed a hand on her chest to feel the thundering of her heart. She laid her other hand on the wall to steady herself.

Yeru hadn't mentioned Whute's name to Sciona.

She was going to include it in the report but she was sure she never mentioned it in her retelling. So how had Scholar Sciona known Whute *by name*? Perhaps she was already known as a member of the cult? Then how had Whute been able to infiltrate the site if they knew of her? Whute had glaring white hair and was hard to miss.

"It must have been one of the other scholars," Yeru whispered to herself. One of them must have told Sciona of Whute.

Unless the head scholar was involved.

If that was the case then Yeru would have more than the library to investigate. She glanced over her shoulder towards the study and then hurried out of the palace.

Yeru wanted nothing more than to drop into her soft bed and sleep away all the thoughts and aches. But she had someone to see first.

Soft singing came from her childhood home as Yeru made her way through to the kitchen. Her mother had her back to Yeru, steam pouring from the pot in front of her. The sweet scent of vegetable stew filled the room. Yeru couldn't help the smile that crept onto her face as she listened to the out of tune humming and watched as her mother wafted away the billowing steam. The warmth of home and family bled into Yeru and relaxed her muscles more than any soft pillow would have done.

Yeru cleared her throat. Her mother stilled and then spun around.

"Yeru!" She lurched forward and hugged her. "I had heard that some scholars had returned. I had hoped…" She drew back teary eyed. "I made some stew, just in case."

Yeru laughed. "Thank you." Her stomach growled. "As always you know what I need before I seem to. But I have something important to ask you before we sit down to eat."

Her mother furrowed her brow. "Of course. What is it?"

"Where was father last sighted?"

ACKNOWLEDGMENTS

Yeru originally played only a small part in the outline for *The Black Mantle* but once I got into drafting the book she demanded more page time. As her part became more substantial, I knew she was a character I wanted to come back to. I was also itching to explore more of the library of Nenelan before *Storm of Shadows*. And so the result was this novella. I love writing from Yeru's perspective and this isn't the last we will see of her...

But like any book, the name on the cover does little to convey the amount of people that helped bring this story to life.

Firstly, I want to thank my beta reader team whose early comments strengthened the story. And my ARC reader team who shared their experience with all who would listen.

My patrons who help fund these books. Including high tier patrons; Brett, Scott, Sophia, Daniela and Don.

My cover artist, Chris, who did an amazing job capturing the spooky atmosphere of the library of Nenelan and some of the horrors it contains.

My editor, Sarah Chorn, who continually makes me a better writer.

My family for their continued support. From being my first readers to just wanting the pretty covers, I couldn't do it without you all.

And lastly, the readers. Without readers, stories are nothing but mad ramblings. It's the reader who imagines the world and the characters and makes them real.

So thank you for making my story real.

ABOUT THE AUTHOR

Andrew Watson lives on the outskirts of Edinburgh where he rambles about made up people and places. He has a first class degree in Digital Media from Edinburgh Napier University and currently works as a freelance video editor and author. Andrew can also be found on YouTube and Instagram where he jumps around excitedly shouting about books.

Follow Andrew at:
andrew-watson.co.uk
@the_fools_tale

www.ingramcontent.com/pod-product-compliance
Lightning Source LLC
Chambersburg PA
CBHW061455210726
48287CB00007B/2524